WOMEN
DREAMING

TRANSLATED BY

WOMEN DREAMING

SALMA

MEENA KANDASAMY

TILTED AXIS PRESS

CAST OF CHARACTERS

Subaida, first married to *Shahul*, then after his passing, *Dawood*. They had a son, *Hasan*, and a daughter, *Parveen*.

Hasina, married to *Iqbal*. Their son *Rahim* was married to Parveen.

Asiyamma, mother to *Meharunnissa* (*Mehar*), and grandmother to *Sajida* (*Saji*) and *Ashraf*. Mehar was married to Hasan.

Sabiamma, a neighbour.

Sulaiamma, another neighbour, married to *Hanifa Hazrat* (cleric and village elder).

Amina, Subaida's great-aunt, who was born blind, and never married.

Nafeesa, Parveen's collaborator and family friend.

Jessima (*Jessi*), Sajida's friend. Her mother was also Mehar's childhood friend.

Khadija, Hasan's second wife.

Habibullah (*Habi*), Mehar's second husband.

PROLOGUE

Parveen runs as though her head is falling apart. Seeing Amma, Hasan and a few others chase her, she runs even faster. The panic of being captured makes her run without paying heed. She runs bounding across walls, past open grounds, she runs and runs...

Waking suddenly out of this nightmare, Parveen was very relieved that no one had caught her. Drenched in sweat, lazy and reluctant to get out of bed, she started thinking about the nature of her dream, what she could recollect of it, the dregs of an earlier life that tormented her now in the form of fantasy. She hated it. She pinched herself to make sure that she had really got away – and that made her overjoyed – then she once again raided her memories.

Meanwhile, downstairs... 'Her mother has come to visit Rahim's wife,' Hasina heard the violent disdain in Iqbal's voice. Absorbing her husband's words, Hasina gathered her loose hair, tied it up in a bun and slowly made her way out of her bedroom. Because she could not see anyone in the living room, she shouted, 'Parveen, Parveen,' her voice loud enough to display her authority as mother-in-law.

Parveen shouted back, 'Maami, here I come,' as she rushed down the stairs. Hasina saw Subaida trailing behind her daughter. Responding to Subaida's muted salaam with a loud and prolonged 'wa 'alaykum al-salaam,' Hasina sat down on the sofa.

When Subaida asks her how she is doing, her tone is reverential, its politeness exaggerated. Hasina's cold response – 'By the grace of Allah there is no dearth of wellness here' – comes across as slightly menacing. Although Subaida is upset that Hasina hasn't asked her to take a seat, she hesitantly stoops to perch on a corner of the sofa.

Parveen is annoyed and angered by her mother-in-law's tone and manner, but she quickly pacifies herself, refusing to show any sign of being perturbed.

'You took the stairs to be with your daughter without first paying your respects to me,' Hasina remarked.

Subaida, registering the reason for Hasina's displeasure, attempts to placate her: 'You were sleeping, that's why I went to talk with Parveen. It has been two weeks since I saw my daughter, you see, so I was very eager...'

This makes Parveen even angrier, to watch her mother plead and try to make peace in such a cringing act of deference.

Perhaps because Hasina had just woken from a nap, her face appeared to be bloated. She had not parted her jet-black hair, merely tied it up into a loose knot, not a hint of grey visible. Parveen compared her mother's veiled head; most of Amma's hair had gone white although both women were of the same age.

'Here, I have brought some snacks,' Subaida extended a bag that she had brought with her towards Hasina, who rejected it casually.

'Why? Who is there to eat them here?'

Parveen ground her teeth in anger – this was all too much to take.

'So, what happened to your promise of buying a car for us? This Eid or the next one?'

Parveen caught the sarcasm in Hasina's sudden barb. She looked towards her mother to see how she would react.

Parveen could not forget that this was the same Hasina who on the day of Parveen's marriage to her son had said, 'She is not your daughter – from this day, she will be my daughter, she will ease my pain of not having given birth to a girl.' She wondered if her mother, too, was ruminating on something similar that Hasina had told them in the past…

'It has been three months since the nikah. When are you going to make good on your promise? Your daughter doesn't understand the first thing about how to conduct herself. She appears to be unfit for any sort of domestic work, as if she was a college-educated girl. Even after I've got a daughter-in-law, I'm the one stuck in the kitchen.'

Subaida regretted having come here. Parveen was meanwhile chastised by Hasina: 'Why are you standing here like a tree – go and fetch some tea for the both of us.'

Parveen moved towards the kitchen. She was curious to know what excuse her mother was going to provide for the demand of a car – but she also knew that she did not have the strength to listen to her spineless words. They must not have promised a car. Why should they have sought an alliance like this? What was wrong with her? Why did they arrange this wedding? She understood nothing.

She filtered the tea into a tumbler. She carefully stirred only half a spoon of sugar in her mother-in-law's cup, knowing that she had to keep an eye on her sugar intake.

Though Parveen had eagerly awaited her mother's arrival, her foremost instinct now was that Amma should leave here immediately. She had wanted to share as many things with her as possible, but now she decided not to confide in her at all. She only wanted her mother to return home peacefully.

With shaking hands, she extended the cup of tea towards her mother-in-law, then served Amma, looking at her intently for some clue.

Hasina, taking a sip and grimacing, remarked: 'Hmm, it's too sweet. Why have you poured so much sugar into this? There's nothing you can do properly. In three months, you have not even learnt how much sugar to add in your mother-in-law's tea. Go, add some milk to my cup and bring it back.'

Her harsh tone made Parveen feel crushed. She worked out that her mother's response about the car must have displeased Hasina. She could see from her mother-in-law's face how embittered and angry she felt.

The house wore a dreadful silence.

Parveen's mother finished her tea and got up to leave. In that dreary living room, Amma stood forlorn, like a beggar, and Parveen felt again that she must leave immediately. She fought hard to prevent the words in her mouth that were waiting to burst forth, restraining herself with great measure. Quietly, she took her mother aside, 'Why do you come here to be humiliated? Go home now.'

In the next few months, when Parveen had been branded an infertile woman and sent back to her parental home, she was actually relieved. When the village started to look at her with sympathy, she realized the full extent to which she was considered a failure. She realized that even worse than the shame of infertility was the shame attached to separation and divorce – society, after all, did not seek any explanations in its appraisal. She, too, sympathized with her situation. If she'd been educated and armed with a degree like her classmates Sabitha or Prabha, she would not have had to go and live in another man's house as a slave and subsequently be kicked out after being labelled infertile because she could not provide her in-laws with a car.

She felt depressed when she realized there was a difference between leaving a marriage on your own terms and being sent back by your husband and his family. She waited for a day when this shame would not invade every fibre of her being.

—

Half-asleep, Meharunnissa looked at the clock. It was 11.30 p.m. and she was worried that her husband was not home yet. She wondered what he was doing so late into the night. The shop would have closed at nine. What was he doing afterwards? She went to the bathroom, then came back and lay down on the bed. She was still very tired. This was the third abortion. For the procedure, she and her mother had secretly visited the family doctor in town and to make sure that no one caught wind of it, she'd spent the next few days in her mother's house. She could not tell her mother-in-law that she was bleeding and healing and unable to cook and clean in this post-operative state. Even when she'd spend a single day in bed, recovering from a cold or a virus of some kind, Subaida would throw dirty glances at her. She did not like to see her daughter-in-law idling away. Wracked with all this guilt, Mehar could only eat very little. How could she afford the luxury of eating in bed having terminated a pregnancy without anyone's knowledge?

If Subaida came to know about the abortion, she would scold her mercilessly. How could she know that her son disliked using condoms? Or was this even something that could be revealed to her? Mehar hadn't confided in her own mother, after all.

When Mehar had first realized her menstrual cycle was delayed, and told Hasan, he'd said, 'Let's keep the child. It's a sin to abort in Islam.'

She had wept bitterly. 'I cannot manage. I already

have these two. And you don't even let me use birth control.'

'Don't you know that it is not permissible to use contraception in Islam? If you do so without my knowledge because your mother is putting ideas into your head, you will only receive a talaq from me.' With that single threat, he'd silenced her.

The next day she had gone to her mother in tears. Her mother reached for every possible slur she could summon to curse Hasan for using her daughter's unblemished body so pitilessly, but she kept her arrows to herself.

'Who in this day and age does not use contraception? Do these laws apply only to him?' she said, blowing her nose. 'If you sleep with him again, I'm going to give you a beating.'

After Hasan's admonishment over the first abortion, Mehar never again breathed a word to him if her periods were delayed.

First, she would simply ask her mother-in-law, 'I'd like to go to my mother's house for a week, may I go?'

Subaida never objected to it. 'Why only for a week, go for ten days, even, and enjoy yourself. It's only the next street – it's not as if you have to take the trouble of going there by car.' So she would wave the green flag. After that there would be no need for

Mehar even to ask her husband – she would merely inform Hasan that she was going and she would leave.

The next day, in order to not rouse anyone's suspicion, she would say to her husband and mother-in-law that little Sajida had a fever, and that she had to take her to the doctor. She would then leave for the procedure, her mother accompanying her.

Her mother's lament would promptly begin in the car, and take at least ten days to subside.

—

The image of Shahul swinging from the noose came to her in a nightmare, and Subaida awoke startled and anxious. 'Allah, why are you ruining my mind,' she muttered and reclined against the wall. Her sari, which hung on the clothesline, fluttered under the ceiling fan.

She did not want to think about those memories, yet she could not avoid how they crept into the corners of her subconscious.

Before her marriage, she had heard the whispers and laughs, the comments about how effeminate Shahul's gait was. But since the day she'd been born, her marriage to him had been fixed. When the time came, Subaida's mother had her reservations: 'Our son-in-law's behaviour and mannerisms do not seem right...' She was afraid to discuss the subject at length with her husband.

'Why?' he would say, 'You don't want to give your daughter in marriage to my sister's son?'

Her mother remained silent. 'Oh no, it's nothing like that...'

'We have only one daughter, and my sister has only one son. There's a lot of property between the two of us. This will be a perfect fit.' He would say this with so much pride that it would quell Subaida's mother's fears. Subaida was not yet at an age where she understood the mysteries of matrimony.

She was married when she was fourteen and went to live with Shahul and his mother – that is, her paternal aunt – who were very kind to her.

Shahul would bring Subaida something to eat every day. He would also buy her earrings, bangles and other little trinkets from the bazaar. She liked him a lot. Her mother who lived one street away would visit her daily. 'Did anything special happen?' her mother would ask her, and she would reply, bemused, 'No, not really.'

One day, after her mother and her aunt had been whispering among themselves, her mother finally asked her, *kulichiya*, have you bathed? Subaida did not understand. She blinked and said, 'Yes.'

'No, not that bath, what an idiot!'

Subaida pondered deeply over the significance of this exchange. She intended to ask Shahul about bathing that evening, but fell asleep before he came home.

In the middle of the night, she was woken by a rustling noise. She had hung her sequinned sari on the clothesline as her mother had always advised her to. She'd intended to air it for an evening before folding it and putting it away in her cupboard for future use. Now she watched Shahul remove the delicate fabric and take it in his arms. Curious, she observed him take her blouse in his hands next, and enter into the nearby room. She could not contain her surprise. She was simultaneously dazed and confused. Subaida summoned up the courage to get out of bed. She took soft steps and stood outside the door of that room; it had been bolted from the inside, so she looked through the keyhole.

To her surprise, Shahul was wearing her sari and blouse. He was standing in front of a small mirror, looking at himself with immense warmth and affection! Subaida felt her head reel. Gripped by fear for her husband's sanity, she quickly went back to bed and lay there with her eyes open. A little while later, she felt him enter the room and lie down next to her. He slept as if nothing out of the ordinary had occurred.

The next morning, when she decided to observe him closely, he seemed to appear as normal...

Meanwhile, her mother and aunt had grown tired of asking her about the 'bathing'. Presented with an opportunity when her aunt was not around, she asked her neighbour Kanisha about it.

Kanisha could not hold back her surprise. 'Oh, you idiot! You are fourteen years old and you still don't know!'

But she had not understood – despite the many, many times her aunt and her mother had brought up the subject. Now she wondered how Kanisha could have grasped the meaning of this mysterious word the very first time she mentioned it. She asked her with wide-eyed wonder: 'What are you saying? Do you really know what *kulichiya* is?'

'Why? Has your husband not said anything to you? Why do you ask me, instead of asking him?'

Kanisha said all this in jest, but when she heard a door open and the approaching footsteps of Subaida's aunt, she scampered off.

'Who is that? Is it that Kanisha? If one is not around, it's enough for such people to invent stories. They'll lose no time in ruining a family,' saying so, Subaida's aunt asked her to fetch a pitcher of water. Subaida wondered how much her mother-in-law had heard, and if perhaps she had rat ears.

Three days later, Shahul had hung himself. Subaida's innocent question had been enough to cause the whole village to talk about him, leading to Shahul taking his own life.

When Subaida thought about how clueless she had been at that age, she was always overcome with disbelief.

CHAPTER 1

Sajida tried to remember the names she knew of the colourful flowers that were strewn along the road on the way back from school. Mullai, malli, December, kanakambaram, she hummed their names to herself as she sprinted home.

Thinking that perhaps she could cheer her mother a little by presenting her with some flowers, she scooped up the ones that were not muddied. She knew that the smallest things could make her mother happy. If Aththa got her a new sari, she would be happy for a week. It was even enough just to tell her that the food she made was very tasty. Of the tricks that her father had mastered in the art of fooling her mother, this was perhaps the simplest.

What could the time be? Could it be four o'clock? Sajida grew sad when she realized that Aththa would probably already be home. If he was at home, it was enough to only be a pair of ears. There would be no need for her eyes, her brain or her limbs to carry any sort of function on their own accord.

What is the need for a girl to watch TV, why not read the Quran?

Why is a girl sleeping in the morning instead of reciting the fajr prayers?

Why are you laughing? Should girls laugh as you do?

Why do you run?

Why do you play?

Why can't you show some patience instead of all this anger?

Mehar, look at your daughter, teach your daughter to have some respect for her elders.

Teach her morals.

Teach her to pray.

These would be the only words that she would hear. How to escape from all of this? Seated on the toilet – a precious moment of respite and solitude – Sajida would search in vain for an answer. The only way out would be to get married. What her mother had to endure was even worse. She wondered if perhaps her mother had become used to all this after all these years.

Approaching the house now, she was shocked to see that the front door had been left wide open. Her mother usually remained behind locked doors all day long, since Aththa believed it was improper for unaccompanied women to be outside. Even if she made the mistake of glancing out at the street, her father would come to know of it somehow and come and shout at her.

Once, their neighbour Sabiamma encouraged her mother to venture out and visit the dargah with her. They could light some lamps, she said, then pray and stroll back home leisurely, enjoying the cool breeze on their faces. Her mother accompanied Sabiamma happily and came back home before Aththa returned – she assumed that the burqa she was wearing would have prevented anyone from identifying her.

But then, Sabiamma had told her husband Sadiq that Mehar had joined her on the visit to the dargah. He, letting out his long-suppressed bitterness, had informed Hasan straight away. Betraying the confidence of his wife and Mehar, Sadiq lectured Hasan just as Hasan had lectured him before: 'When women of the village go to the dargah, you quote a thousand hadiths and censure them, asking them what a woman is doing in a man's burial place – how are you going to justify your own wife going there today and lighting lamps?'

Sajida vividly remembers the scolding and beatings that her mother received that night. She had remained silent and motionless under her bed sheets as she heard her father reproach her mother. *I'm trying to reform those who choose the wrong path and bring them towards ibaddat – and you are trying to ruin my reputation?* That long terrifying night, punctuated by her mother's desperate sobs, Sajida went to sleep plotting her escape from her father.

'Hey Sajida, are you returning home from school only now?' the voice of her neighbour Sabiamma broke her reverie. She nodded and stepped inside. Her exams were due to start the next day so she planned to revise long into the night.

As she walked into the living room, her mother ran towards her and held her in an embrace. She burst out crying, 'Your father has dropped a rock on our heads.' Without fully understanding the import of these words, Sajida wrapped her arms around her mother's neck and wept with her.

CHAPTER 2

The house was calmer than ever. Mehar sat in her room wondering if this was a good thing or a bad thing. A layer of cream was forming on the cup of tea that her mother had made for her. She was yet to reconcile with the shock. On the one hand, she was concerned about the future. On the other hand, there was a feeling of immense relief, of having escaped something dreadful. The sound of the call to prayer came from far away. Before, whenever she heard it, she would hastily pull the headscarf over herself. Now, for whatever reason, it annoyed her. She felt as if offering prayers was no longer necessary.

I'm a man. I can marry as many times as I want. The law lets me do that – the arrogance of Hasan's words had lodged itself in her ears. From the next room, her mother's protestations echoed against the walls. Sajida and Ashraf were asleep.

Mehar was delighted that Allah Himself had given

her the opportunity to escape a miserable hell. If that were the case, she thought it essential to say her prayers of gratitude to Allah the Saviour.

In earlier times, the women of the village would only wear white headscarves. She, too, would wear a loose white cotton headscarf if she had to leave the house to attend someone's marriage or someone's wake. It was only after Hasan returned from Saudi Arabia that his dogma had become unbearable. *From now onwards, wear the purdah – even your eyes should not be visible to the outside world.* He had brought the purdah himself all the way from Makkah.

Before, at least some of the jewellery she wore or the sari that she had draped was visible. She felt happy to show these things to other women and listen to their compliments. After she started wearing the purdah, it became pointless to wear beautiful saris.

Every morning, upon waking, her husband would set out to write the hadith of the day on the community blackboards kept in every street. What he wrote was always some chastisement aimed at women, whether related to their conduct, their obligations to their husband and family, or their moral infirmities. At times it would irritate her greatly. Did people write such things in the olden days? Even her mother would note, 'Your husband is so worried about the world's moral code, does he mean to reform the entire village? Even the women in the neighbourhood are mocking him!'

In a way, Meharunnissa felt that she had attained her freedom. Now, she was not going to live in his house, under his rules. There was some comfort to be found in this.

CHAPTER 3

As she lay in bed, Mehar tried to reason whether her decision to leave him was solely because of his second marriage. Only her heart knew the truth. The day after she came to her mother's home, she told her flatly: 'I will not live with him again, we have to seek the khula.'

It did not appear as if her decision either shocked or upset her mother. As if she agreed with her daughter's intention of asking for a divorce, she sat down calmly beside her. The two women sat in silence, an intermittent tubercular cough occasionally ringing out from within Mehar's mother's burqa.

Mehar knew the chain of thoughts that was running through her mother's head: *This sinning bastard, my innocent daughter... He married her when she was barely a child and as if it was not enough to leave her body wounded and savaged, he has the gall to marry a second time! May he perish in hell.*

Asiyamma coughed loudly. 'Was there a single day, my child, when you could step out of the house? All the time, it was prayer, ibaddat! He ruined my daughter, never showed her any of the world's pleasures, kept her locked up, and now he has married another woman—' her mother raged on and on, her words already starting to tire Mehar.

What was the use of crying over spilt milk? Why did her mother have to lament when she knew Mehar was herself unhappy with him? Was this not a blessing in disguise since now he could no longer lord over her? Would life not be peaceful now?

All the village women would wear lipstick on festive occasions, at a wedding or Eid celebrations. On the one occasion she wore it, her husband had called Mehar a prostitute a thousand times.

I am a member of the Tablighi Jamaat. From now on, you need not go to pay condolences for a death in anyone's family, nor to the ritual observation on the third day. You must not deviate from the true path of the religion, you must stay at home and recite the fatiha.

Even Subaida would wonder where her son got all these rules and regulations from, for how could she not recite the fatiha on Wednesday or the twenty-seventh day of the month? She'd been doing so her entire life! She would complain endlessly.

When she was not allowed to make a donation to some cause or other, she sobbed and sobbed. 'The whole village is feasting on kandhuri rice and curry but this man is not even letting us taste it!' She prayed to God to bestow her son with some good sense.

While the women of the village wore light cotton or chiffon saris as a matter of pride, Hasan would buy thick polyester ones for the women in his household. *These village women, they lack any propriety or morality and drape their saris so that their whole body is exposed. It would be better if they went about bare-assed instead.*

Subaida would refuse to wear the polyester saris! 'If my sari is thin, at least it will not be suffocating, it will rest easily and it will be breathable. In my old age, I cannot carry this heavy polyester. At this point in my life, who will stare at this old lady's breasts! Tell your wife to wear them if you must!'

Mehar treasured her lightest saris. Her mother had selected them with great care, and since her thirteenth birthday, had amassed about fifty saris as part of her dowry. To guests who would visit, Asiya would proudly say: 'I'm keeping some of the finest Indian saris for my daughter. Over two years, I have collected fifty saris. If I do not get her married now, in two more years, I will have a hundred!' Mehar thought of her mother boasting about this fact in front of those who came for the fatiha a day before the wedding.

For a couple of years, Hasan behaved as a man ought to. But after his two-year stint in Saudi Arabia, he forbade Mehar to wear even a single one of her thin saris.

Mehar sighed. She reminded herself of all the reasons why she should divorce him. She consoled herself with the thought that God had shown her the way out of a trap that she could never have escaped otherwise. But just as her sister-in-law Parveen had been labelled a failure, so she, too, would inevitably become one in the eyes of the community.

CHAPTER 4

Hasan simply could not come to terms with what he was meant to do, once he realized that Mehar was not coming back.

What did it matter to a woman how a man lived? Islam did not consider it a sin for a man to marry four times, he thought to himself. Just thinking about Mehar filled him with aversion. She was an idiot who knew nothing. Since the day he had married her, his hatred towards her had multiplied. He was left with nothing except the feeling of living with a corpse. Perhaps things would improve with time, he'd thought, since she was only fifteen years old when he married her. But she proved to be utterly incompetent at anticipating his needs.

That morning, after the fajr prayers, Hanifa Hazrat had taken him aside. 'Yesterday, your mother-in-law came to my home,' he said, 'She gave me notification of khula, your wife's intention to divorce. I just wanted to inform you...' The hesitation in his voice suggested that he was aware of the seriousness of the situation.

'What arrogance! Fucking bitch!' Hasan grumbled to himself, then quickly asked Allah's forgiveness for swearing.

'Well, what can be done now... For the first time, in the history of this community, something that has never come to pass before.' His face revealed his worries.

'I spoke to the jamaat too. Sadaq is your uncle, after all. He says that if we allow this to happen it will set a precedent for every other woman in the village. He'd like to avoid it, but what to do?'

Hasan's blood boiled. He bit his tongue, furious.

Knowing that any attempt to talk to Hasan was like banging one's head against a wall, Hanifa Hazrat spoke the bare minimum. Then, in a rush of urgency, he asked, 'Why did you marry for the second time, brother? That was not right.'

'I've only done what the religion permits,' replied Hasan coldly. 'The law allows me to marry four women. I have the boldness to do that and the means to support my wives. What is wrong with that?'

Hasan's reply only frustrated Hanifa Hazrat further.

'That was in the olden days. And more importantly, you must remember what the law says – that you must first obtain your first wife's permission to marry; next, that you can marry another woman only if you can treat both wives equally and with no difference in your comportment. Will all this work out in our modern times? And did you ask Mehar's permission to take a second wife? And, then, who is this new girl?' His curiosity betrayed itself.

'Permission!' Hasan untied the lungi wrapped around his waist and retied it with exasperation. 'Which woman will accept it, Hazrat? You are asking me to respect her and obtain her permission. I am earning a good salary. Islam allows for four wives. They are doing just that in the Arab countries. I've married under halal law. What do you have to say to that?' He argued so loudly and vociferously that Hanifa felt a bit taken aback.

He conceded some ground. 'Okay. That is your wish. Now I have received this petition. What are we supposed to do? She has asked for it – it's not like I'm in favour of it. That is all.'

Hasan tied his kerchief on his head and left the mosque.

Hanifa could see that the arrogance in Hasan's tone was missing from his stride.

Hasan did not understand what the fuss about his second marriage was. His mother Subaida had not uttered a single word to him the whole week. His daughter Sajida had left along with Mehar – she had refused even to speak with him on the phone. Then his sister Parveen was giving him the silent treatment. Out on the street, he heard the hawkers crying, 'nungu, nungu,' weaving along on their bicycles. Sajida loved eating nungu. Hasan wanted to buy some and send them to her grandmother's place, but he quickly dropped that idea.

He missed the sweet cajoling voice of his daughter – but instead of blaming himself for the situation, he directed his anger towards Mehar. 'Stupid, unlucky bitch, she has not even finished sixth standard and she has the cheek to divorce me. Has she even any idea where her next meal will come from?'

And then he thought how he had grossly underestimated her. She would cry for two days and then she would settle down to passively accept the situation – that had been his calculation.

Filled with such conflicting thoughts, he started making his way home. He greeted Razak, who half-heartedly returned his salaam, and Hasan could glean the hatred that lay underneath. Even the youngsters of Sheikh Dawood's house seemed to regard him with contempt now. Hasan wondered if he was projecting his own anxieties.

By the time he reached home, he realized that he had lost both Mehar and Sajida and that he no longer had any control over their lives.

CHAPTER 5

Subaida felt her throat had dried up from all her weeping. She had not eaten since morning and, in any case, her daughter-in-law Mehar was not around to cook. The family's honour, their name, reputation – everything had been burnt to the ground. What was the point of living! With her arms outstretched, she broke into open-mouthed lament, 'I only gave birth to two children. What pleasure did I derive from this life, God, getting married to an old man as his second wife? Now both my children's lives have been ruined, does this seem just?'

She was terrorized by the prospect of what the neighbours and relatives would say to Mehar initiating divorce proceedings – after all, when Parveen was sent home everyone had said uncharitable things.

Why did Hasan's mind have to tread this path when he had a wife and children to think of – couldn't he live with them for the sake of his family even if he did not like his wife? Now he would pay the price for all this sin – he would be ruined!

Subaida felt worn out. She thought back to the days of her marriage to the old Dawood bhai, after the passing of Shahul.

She remembered crying as a young girl, newly widowed, 'You are marrying me to this old man as if there is no food in this house to feed me?' Her mother, too, had wept and begged her, 'No, my dear girl. A woman must live with her husband. How long can we support you? After us, who will be there to look after you? Everyone in this village knows that you are a virgin. But who else will come forward to be your second husband, you tell me?'

The price she paid for her first marriage was the life she lost through her second. But all her sadness and grief had been absolved by the birth of Parveen and Hasan. Her mother had been right; when Dawood died, she was happy to live her life with just her children. But it seemed as if God was not happy even with this arrangement.

'Allah, you have dismantled my family and mauled this little sparrow's nest.'

No one was at home now to hear her cries.

CHAPTER 6

Sulaiamma tentatively opened the door and peeked inside. The door had not been bolted. Softly, she said, 'Asiya?' then, 'Mehar,' a little louder, but nobody could be seen. Again, she shouted, 'Hey, Asiya!'

From behind the clothesline at the end of the house, Asiya emerged. 'What?' she asked, a little sharply.

'Nothing. I just came by – to see you all...' Sulaiamma's voice faltered.

Asiya was having none of it. 'Okay, now you have seen us. You may leave.'

It did not appear as if anyone could speak to her. Sulaiamma quickly scrutinized the verandah to see if she could at least catch sight of Mehar passing by. Asiya chided her: 'What are you looking for? She is asleep. No one need come by to meet my daughter or enquire about her sorrow. She is fine – please do not provoke things.'

With this, Asiya stalked off. Sulaiamma started back towards her own home. 'What bloody arrogance. Damn widow, came to give her my good counsel – but…' Of course, Sulaiamma thought, men make mistakes. It was for women to bear with them. Had Hasan done something no other man had done in the entire world? For that, Mehar would be ignoring the fate of her two children and asking for khula? She would ruin this whole village!

As she approached her house, she heard the voice of Hanifa Hazrat. 'What happened? Did they say anything?'

'No. They did not even let me enter the house,' Sulaiamma's face shrank with shame.

Knowing that his wife's undertaking had failed, Hanifa Hazrat made his way towards the mosque. He reasoned to himself that whether or not Hasan agreed to the khula was immaterial. If the wife had decided, so be it; there was provision for that in the law. This was the way of the Lord.

The call to prayer that reverberated in the distance seemed to harden his resolve.

—

When Parveen returned from her in-laws', Hasan was bolting around like a mad man.

'I will bite his throat, that bastard,' he swore at his brother-in-law. It was left to Parveen to pacify him, 'Leave it bhai, he is a useless fellow...'

Gradually, Parveen became extremely irritated by the rules and regulations that she found she had to subscribe to in Hasan's house. She was seized by anxiety: how would she and her mother spend the rest of their days living with a man who constantly preached the hadith and ibaddat? She longed to seal her ears with wax just so she didn't have to listen to his ceaseless talk. Her childhood home had become at once a mosque and a prison. Advice, advice, unceasing advice to women... the steps one must follow to live a good life, to reach heaven – women were subject to all of it. Compared to Hasan's home, Parveen felt that even her covetous husband's house was a better place!

When had Hasan adopted this persona? She grew tired of thinking this through – had it all been a Saudi influence? When she received the polyester saris and the black burqas just like her mother and Mehar, perhaps she should have considered her future more seriously. She was afraid of developing a great hatred towards her brother and her religion because of his constant preaching. After all, she said her prayers five times a day and read the Quran; but the unyielding and antiquated rules her brother insisted upon were entirely unacceptable to her.

Here, Parveen. Allah will grant you great rewards in the afterlife. Forget what is going on in this one. It is nothing. Pray, observe your fasts, increase your ibaddat, do not watch TV, relinquish the vulgarities of life, search for the path to heaven: what do you say to this?

She thought of Mehar and felt great pity for her. How had she put up with him? She realized that his actions and utterances were mixed with the arrogance that comes from being a man. Resolute in her decision not to spend the rest of her life at his mercy she had told her mother, 'I cannot bear to stay in this house any longer – I feel suffocated!'

Subaida looked at her daughter, a worried expression on her face. 'Where will you go?'

'I will stay with Nanni. She only lives on the next street.'

Subaida could not prevent her. She could not understand the extent to which life in the house was oppressive. When Parveen saw her mother was agitated, she brushed it aside as a sign of the older woman's rigidity. Her great-aunt Amina had no children, so Parveen moved in with her.

Parveen felt unable to attend any village ceremonies or festivities. The women's sympathetic looks made her life hell. She was offended. At least the home of her great-aunt felt like a refuge she could claim, and it lacked such tensions. Often, she would wonder how Mehar and Sajida would escape the tyranny of Hasan in the coming days. She thought of their parallel lives time and again.

—

'What have you come to see? That my daughter's life is broken, that she sits in a corner, that she is weeping?' The shrill tone of Asiyamma's words pierced Parveen and caused her to turn. Asiyamma was beating her own face and chest with her hands as she wept.

Parveen made her way towards Mehar and sat next to her.

Sajida and Ashraf, who woke on hearing their grandmother's cries, hugged their mother and buried their faces in her lap, scrunching the fabric of her sari in their mouths.

'Please do not cry, it is upsetting the children,' Parveen said, though she was aware that her words would not bring consolation to anyone.

'Your brother has thrown some thunder bolts over these innocent heads. Now they have become orphans. He did not want to look at their little faces and instead went in search of a new cunt. He will be ruined.' Though these were vulgar words of reproach, shouting in this manner seemed to relieve Asiya of her fury and hatred. She had a shrivelled body, as if only her bones remained; her hair was matted and tangled, and her skin had been battered by tuberculosis. Mehar's face appeared to lack any emotion – and the fear of the coming days seemed not to have gripped her yet. Her eyes were wide, as if she was taking in everything that was happening around her.

Parveen wondered if just like herself, Mehar was a little glad to have escaped Hasan's tyranny, but she could not judge too clearly yet.

'Even a single day, could she have worn a sari that she liked?' Asiyamma continued, 'Could she have worn make-up? Look at all the women of the village who are of her age – how they wear new clothes, how they make themselves up – did she ever have any such pleasure?

'Like a servant she had to cook, feed him, sleep… A fire burns in my stomach!' Asiya hit herself again and again, and wept with great expression. An urge to leave this place crept up on Parveen – but she sat patiently, unsure of what was to be done.

It would be easy for her to escape, but how would Mehar get away from all this? It was as if she had jumped from the frying pan into the fire.

To rectify the situation, she held the children and

took their hands in hers. She put on her headscarf.

'Mehar, give it some time. Patience,' her voice urged, pleading.

'My daughter is innocent, untouched. I had her married when she was just fifteen, and now at thirty, she is reduced to nothing, sitting in a corner of the house! My daughter never had a moment of pleasure, not even a single day, because of that bastard! Who knows what will become of her?'

Once again, tormented by the howling voice and the just words it bleated, Parveen hurried out.

CHAPTER 7

Her head resting in Parveen's lap, Sajida was over-come with sorrow. She remembered her father's face with great regularity; indeed, it had been five months since she had spoken with him. His voice – the voice that used to call her *Sajidaaaammaaa* – had vanished forever. Never again would she hear that loving voice. And even if she were to hear it, she knew she would not like it.

There were so many questions to which she did not have the answers. Why did he marry again? Would she ever know what made him do it? Whatever the reason, it was unacceptable. How could he leave Sajida and her brother? How could he spend his days without talking to them, without looking at them?

If Ashraf happened to see his father out on the streets somewhere, he followed him for a distance and then returned home, sombre. Sajida had stopped speaking with her father because she knew that her mother would not like it.

She often felt that she would go mad listening to her mother and grandmother go on lamenting without pause. But there was no choice, for that was where her loyalties lay. She felt as if she could still hear the howls and coughs of her grandmother, raging, raging... In the midst of all this turbulence, she had successfully finished her public exams for the year. Now the stress about results took hold of her.

One day, quite out of the blue, her mother had gone to their school and got a transfer certificate for her and Ashraf. And when asked for a reason she'd said, 'I cannot let him educate them on his expense in a school of his choice.' This was the story that Mariya Teacher had relayed to Sajida.

'Your mother and grandmother are pulling you out of this perfectly good school. And where are they going to enrol you? Are they idiots?' As she heard Mariya Teacher say these words she could not under-stand the intent behind them, but Sajida felt a prickle of anger to hear her teacher say such derogatory things about her mother and grandmother. She, too, had felt that it would be better if she left that school and went away elsewhere.

Besides, everyone at that school had known that Aththa had a second marriage. She remembered how

Sabeena and Shakila had teased her about it. She'd told her mother, 'Send me to a hostel in town so that I can study there. Not here.' Nor did her mother demand another reason from her. 'You can enrol my brother into the nearby school...'

Reliving these strange five months, Sajida blinked her eyes open to look up at her aunt Parveen. When Parveen asked her if she wanted to go back home to her mother, Sajida shook her head and lay down again. She was afraid to go there. The sound of wailing seemed to haunt her. Then she felt that she had no choice but to go back, to witness her mother's pain. So she got up, took her burqa in her hand and started to slip it on.

There was some consolation in the fact that her mother did not cry and howl like her grandmother. It made her wonder if Mehar was putting on a brave face just for the sake of her children. Still, there was consolation, too, in the fact that her mother was strong. Fond memories of good times with her father came to her from time to time. She longed for an occasion when she would sit in the front passenger's seat of the car, next to her father, and they would talk as he drove. She gracefully let go of those memories when she realized such things were no longer possible.

Sajida embraced her aunt and kissed her. Appearing

to understand her difficulties, Parveen Kuppi, too, hugged her with warmth, caressed her hair and kissed her goodbye. Sajida assumed that when Ashraf woke, he would make his own way home.Now she walked down the road in her burqa, feeling a sense of pride and relief when she realized that no one would be able to identify her.

She had reached puberty the very day her mother had first cried to her; the day after her father's second marriage, she had become a woman. Because of all the ongoing commotion, no one did anything to celebrate the occasion of Sajida's first period. Even otherwise, there was not much to expect, since her father did not appreciate such uncultured things. Nor would he have allowed them to mark the event. She knew this for a fact since she had heard her mother worry about it to her grandmother. This made her even sadder.

When the girls of the village who were in her age group reached puberty, there was so much celebration and fanfare. She had been left without any ritual of that sort.

CHAPTER 8

Hasan longed to see Sajida and to speak with her. He no longer had any expectations that she would love him or even talk to him like she had before. He wondered why he had never anticipated the extent to which his children might hate him.

His mother had also told him in no uncertain terms: 'Don't bring your new wife to this house. I will live on my own. I've lived enough being married to an old man, then raising you and Parveen.'

He felt he had committed a mistake in his haste. But what was his mistake? After all, so what if a man married for a second time? And after all, these were the days when women were initiating divorce! He had to remind himself that he was a man – and that fact alone was enough to prevent him from feeling any guilt.

Such were his thoughts as he walked towards the mosque. He saw Rasiq and Siddiq walking in his direction – he had known them from the time of his tablighi work. Seeing them, he expected that they would offer him salaams, but they walked past as if they had not even noticed Hasan. Their behaviour surprised and shocked him. He turned back and shouted, 'Hey, are you blind or what? Walking by without even saying salaam!'

'Is that Hasan machchaan! 'Wa 'alaykum al-salaam! We really did not see you. It is time for kandhuri in our village, so we were just discussing that....'

Hasan understood that they were coming up with lame excuses. 'I see, brothers – I wish you the best. I'm on my way to pray.' He was overcome with an unspeakable grief and shame. He consoled himself that everything was naseeb, just the way the Lord had willed it. But even if Hasan was able to find solace in these thoughts, he remained inconsolable that he could not see his daughter.

They live on the next street. How strong-willed my girl must be to avoid seeing me.

Hamid the shop boy was standing outside the mosque. 'Anna, sir, they are asking for rice and meat from the house – we got a request,' he said. Hasan was annoyed that a simple meal of rice and meat alone was enough for Sajida. He realized that this was because her mother Mehar had been poor when he'd married her.

He was once again reminded of Rasik and Siddiq's behaviour and felt enraged. Until the previous day, they had been brothers, they had worked in the jamaat together – what had caused them to reserve so much hatred towards him.

I did only what was allowed by the law. What was so wrong about that? What problem was it of theirs? On Thursday, they would have to come along with Hasan when the kasthu went through the streets... Hasan would have to see how that would play out.

He wanted to move on and find something else to occupy his mind, but he was filled with a vague feeling of loss.

CHAPTER 9

Several days had passed since Mehar had looked out onto the streets or talked to anyone. She was surprised that she had not yet turned mad. After she had initiated the khula proceedings, Hanifa Hazrat had asked her to wait for a period of four months and ten days. This was the mandatory iddha that she had to observe.

She had no idea how to take life forward. She did not know how many years she would have to spend listening to her mother's racking cough and her endless expressions of grief. Whether morning dawned or not, it was accompanied by Asiyamma's cruel curses and coughing fits. Indeed, she was not yet satisfied with the curses she had already thrown in Hasan's direction.

Mehar wondered how it was possible to blame a man in so many ways. Then she wondered if her mother's pain had made her lose her mind.

Ashraf was nowhere to be seen. Perhaps he had

run away to his father. That's where he would usually run to upon waking. Perhaps that was the reason why her mother was shouting, and having figured this out, Mehar started brushing her teeth. Today she was going to enrol Sajida in another school for the eleventh standard.

A distant relative's son would be visiting. He would accompany Asiya and Sajida to the school – and they would stay in the hostel. Twice, Hasan had sent over mutual relations or neighbours to ask if he could take care of Sajida's schooling. But Mehar could not accept this. She did not yet know her daughter's intentions either.

Deep down, Mehar knew that Sajida's decision to live in a hostel had come about because she was sick of watching the two women cry and curse all day. After all, Sajida had loved her father. But, for the last five months, she'd stopped talking to him. Often, seeing her daughter curled up in bed, Mehar would feel sick to her stomach, afraid of just how much her daughter was yearning for her father.

Perhaps she should let her talk to him, she would think, but her anger would allow no such thing. *If he had thought about the children, would he have married another woman? Why did he have children if he did not care about them?* In this manner, she had rationalized her decisions.

Sajida was asleep and her skirt had ridden up to her thighs. Mehar took care not to wake her as she gently tugged it down. There was sufficient time to leave for school and she wanted Saji to sleep for a little while longer. Had they been living with Hasan, he would have woken everybody up by five in the morning.

Why does the girl have to sleep instead of offering the morning prayers? he would have argued. And Mehar would want to retort: *Yes, she should catch up on all the sleep she will miss when she is older, when she will have to wake up early and work tirelessly for her husband and her mother-in-law.* But even her opinion on something so mundane had to be expressed with the greatest reserve.

Oh! So you are implying that this is how you suffer, working for me and my mother – and using such an opportunity to shamelessly taunt me, he would have said. *Are you going to make a habit of using the morning prayer for such idiotic excuses?* Mehar would be afraid when he spoke like that.

She felt constrained by this small room, the rickety bed and the wheezing cupboards. The walls bore the marks of oil-stained heads, and prayer mats hung along the clothesline. When Mehar considered that she was going to live the rest of her life in this space, she was struck by sadness.

The little shop her father had left behind and the money garnered from renting it might be sufficient for her mother, but it wasn't enough for her. Mehar wanted more from life. She was not yet wholly convinced that keeping the children with her just to prevent them from being with Hasan was in their best interests. When Hanifa Hazrat had asked Hasan to pay some compensation, he had said, 'Was it I who asked for a divorce? She could have considered what would become of the children but that arrogant woman chose not to!'

'Why the hell would I take his money?' she mumbled to herself. A fire burned in her heart, and with it, the conviction that he deserved to be punished even more. 'Even the shame of a divorce has not made him less headstrong!' She marvelled at the rage and bitterness that swelled inside her.

The morning light slid inside the room. She heard a voice greet someone, 'Salaam Maami,' and she listened attentively to figure out who it could be.

When her mother's voice rang out, she realized that this was the man who was here to take her daughter to school. She didn't remember having met him even once. Her mother had told her that his wife had died in a road accident four, five years ago – and since then, he'd lived alone.

For the admission fees at school, she had come up with the money by pledging her jewels.

Asiya asked her, 'Should we spend so much money on educating a girl? That too in a hostel?'

But Saji was adamant. 'I want to study and become a doctor,' she'd said.

Mehar too wanted Saji to be educated and to take up a job. 'If I had been educated beyond the fifth standard that filthy man might not have abandoned me in my middle age. I will educate my daughter as I was not.' She was firm.

She had heard that yesterday he had told Hanifa Hazrat's wife of his plans to put Sajida in a good madrassa so she could study towards becoming an alima. Sulaiamma, as mediator, had broached the topic with Mehar politely but even as she was explaining Hasan's thinking, her throat dried up. She had rightly anticipated the reaction that would follow.

Asiya started screaming, 'Did that bastard send you here?' Sulaiamma didn't stay to listen to the rest of the old woman's tirade, and skulked away.

Mehar had known that Hasan had plans for Sajida to study in a madrassa and get a religious education. *When my daughter comes of age, I will not send her to school – young girls are set on the wrong path in that morally corrupt environment. We should put her in the madrassa for two years so that she can learn ilm, and respect it, then we must marry her to a man who has the same knowledge of religion.* When he spoke like this, it left Mehar enraged.

She mumbled to herself, 'You would try to marry my daughter to a fool like yourself.'

Today, almost as if she was savouring the taste for revenge, she was going to enrol Sajida in a school and later, she would send her to college. It was a matter of pride. It brought her peace of mind to know that he could not tolerate this. It was a cruel sort of peace.

Her mother, Habibullah and Saji returned home late that night after admitting her to a school in town. Asiya, tired and emotional, hugged Sajida and started to weep. Mehar knew she was crying because Sajida was going to leave them all in a few days to stay at boarding school.

Looking in Mehar's direction, Asiya said, 'How long will you spend your days alone? What will you do when I am dead and gone?' Mehar looked at her mother with surprise, trying to figure out her intentions. 'What are you going to do with these two children in times like this? There are so many errands to run, hospital visits, and everyday responsibilities.

You are not even thirty years old.'

Her mother's lengthy explanations, when seen in the yellow light of the veranda, seemed to have brought a surreal glow to her face.

'This Habi is a golden boy. He will be a support to you and the children. Please marry him, my dear.'

The next instant, Mehar felt her mother's cries slide off the walls, sticky and sibilant, and cling to her.

CHAPTER 10

Mehar worried that her mother really had gone mad. Sajida, not understanding anything, slipped away from her grandmother's arms and went towards the bathroom.

The clothes drying on the clothesline at the back of the house rustled in the wind. A couple of lizards scurried across the floor in an attempt to catch their prey; luck was on their side as something or other always landed on their long pink tongues. Mehar sat silently watching the lizards, stupefied.

'I wasn't thinking practically when we gave the khula. But now I realize how much you need a man by your side. I will die at any time – my life hangs by a thread. Don't you need someone to look after you when I am gone? What happiness did you ever enjoy with that wicked man?'

Mehar gently held her mother's hands, 'Amma, are you feeling okay? I'm frightened for you! You're talking like a madwoman...' Her voice exposed Mehar's predicament. How could she look at her mother, her only source of support, as a mad person?

'No, dear child, I am perfectly lucid. I am afraid that I will die, the sorrows of life have become too much to bear all of a sudden. I just don't want to leave you on your own.' Asiya beat her face and her breasts with her outstretched arms as she cried.

Knowing that this was not an appropriate time to talk rationally to her mother, Mehar inched her way backwards and stepped into her own room.

Sajida was baffled. She looked at her mother in utter confusion, then turned her head away. She was delighted to have escaped her fate of attending a madrassa, and happy to have joined a new school. For the first time in many months, she thanked Allah for the separation from her father.

It was because of her father's second marriage that her mother had divorced him. It was because of the divorce that they could escape their father's tyranny. That was why she was not going to the madrassa. That was also why she was going to a school in town. As these thoughts swirled in her little sleepy head, she felt a little consoled.

CHAPTER 11

Parveen placed the simple meal she had prepared for Amina on the dining table and went into her room. Her grandmother would finish the night prayers, then eat dinner, chew the betel leaf, and sleep as and when it suited her.

In her room, Parveen caught her reflection in the mirror. Her face, once beautiful, felt to her ruined by sorrow. Her hair was already greying in places. And she had read in a weekly magazine just this morning that if one did not have regular sexual intercourse, old age would descend very early. At least once a week, the columnist had recommended, and Parveen had laughed to herself. Then she pondered over what she might have done with all that youth and vitality if it was ever in reach.

These days, most of her nights were marked by insomnia. The television seemed to always be blaring romantic scenes, intimate bedroom dialogues that left her aroused. Though it was unpleasant to run through her memories with Rahim, she wondered if she had ever achieved an orgasm with him. For a few days following their marriage they had only kissed and cuddled. Sex could come later.

After some time, she realized that Rahim might have a problem, that everything was not how it was meant to be. She reasoned that perhaps he lacked any experience; it took her a few weeks to realize the difference between inexperience and impotence. Instead of feeling remorseful that he might have placed their relationship under strain, Rahim seemed to be more concerned with ensuring that his wife remain ignorant about his dysfunction.

Even if she might have been willing to understand his situation and live with him despite it, he lacked the maturity to accept that he could not perform; his manhood simply did not let him concede to it. He was eager to use any excuse to send her out of the house, and out of that marriage.

Only Parveen and Rahim knew that the demand for a car was an extended metaphor for his failure in the bedroom. She often wanted to talk to him about the matter open-heartedly. She wanted to tell him that no matter what the trouble was, she would stay with him. She believed it would be better to live with her husband than return home as a discarded bride; she would spend the rest of her days in his home, doing what she could to earn her place there. But it seemed it was of paramount importance to Rahim's ego to hide his deficiency from his own wife.

Even today, she did not blame Rahim. The way he had been brought up, after all, had shaped how he conceived of his masculinity. His mind was unwilling to admit the smallest crack in that image. Of course, it must have soothed his self-worth to reject her and send her back to her family on the grounds of her supposed infertility – but she had accepted all this, taken it into her stride. She realized that if there had been another factor, she would have faced the necessity of having to enter into some other matrimonial relationship at some point in her life.

Before the divorce, when they went to the jamaat to seek counsel, one or two individuals suggested that it would be better to consult a family doctor to discuss the issue of Parveen's fertility and the possibility of treatment to enable her to have children. But Rahim had vehemently opposed these proposals. Parveen had breathed a sigh of relief because she knew that once she'd been labelled infertile, no man in the village would marry her. Her brother, who had promised to gift her husband a car upon their marriage, had returned from Saudi Arabia with the new insight that it was haram to offer dowry.

And now, Parveen found consolation in the fact that she had escaped the fate of living with their mother. Whenever her mother would suggest a second marriage, Parveen would retort a little unfeelingly: 'I do not want to end up like you, as the second wife of a very old man, nor do I want to be married to some widower who already has children so that I can become a maid in someone else's house.' Because it had been decided that Parveen could not bear children, everyone who sought her hand in marriage turned out to be a widower or someone who already had children. When her mother would blame these men for looking for an unpaid nanny, Parveen would laugh bitterly to herself.

But she was lonely. No matter how strong-willed she was – neither her body nor her emotions were willing to listen to her. This was the truth. The sleepless nights continued. Because she could not detach her body's longing through masturbation alone, she had to carry it everywhere she went. She reasoned to herself that not everything had a solution – and proceeded to take off the saris hanging from the clothesline, fold them and place them in the cupboard. There were too many. Her mother never kept much for herself.

'Do I have a husband who will admire me wearing a beautiful sari?' Her mother would say, and she had ended up amassing a large collection for her daughter.

In the distance, Parveen heard a dog bark, and her thoughts turned to Mehar and Sajida. She felt that in some way, Mehar had escaped from Hasan. What good would come of living with such a controlling man? But when she thought about the children, she grew worried.

What a grave mistake you have made, Hasan, she thought to herself. She heard Amina call to her and went to check on her. Amina, sitting on her prayer mat, her head covered, seemed concerned she might have woken Parveen.

'Were you in bed, Parveen? I have misplaced my tasbeeh somewhere – could you please help me find it?'

Parveen found the rosary from under the bed and placed it tenderly in Amina's hands.

'May I take leave?' Parveen asked.

'Yes dear, you must sleep. You will do well, you will live a hundred years,' Amina blessed Parveen, but her voice lacked conviction, as if she knew how meaningless the words were; a gesture, simply, a habit. Parveen went back to her room with a small smile on her face. Amina's door would stay open throughout the night. Parveen wanted to be able to hear her if she called out to her, so she left her own door a little ajar, too.

Parveen estimated that Amina Nanni would be at least seventy years old. Her mother was fifty, so this was more or less a good approximation. What a challenge it must be to live for seventy years as a blind person. Allah!

Because she was blind, she had never married, she could not travel, she could not visit others – she had lived seventy long and uneventful years.

'What is happiness for you, Nanni?' Parveen had asked her once, hesitating. But Amina had replied directly, without skipping a beat: 'Good food, and listening to songs on the radio.'

Parveen would never forget her answer.

CHAPTER 12

Sajida thought of her father. She wondered if he had really forgotten her, as her mother claimed. It was not possible. After all, he used to buy her her favourite chocolate every day and speak with her in the most affectionate manner. She tried to understand how he could bear not having seen or spoken to her for the last four months.

It was also confusing to believe her mother's explanation that Aththa had remarried because he did not like them. Yet, it was only because he was not around that she could go and study in a hostel.

She didn't like this place. Just as her father's sermons and instructions would fill her ears at home, her grandmother's cries and curses oppressed her here. She was counting the days until she could be in the hostel. Ashraf would go and meet their father in the shop or the mosque. Their mother would come to know of it somehow and she would scold him endlessly.

So Sajida did not even dare to ask her brother if her father had said anything about her.

Her classmate Jessima had come home yesterday to visit her. Afraid that she would hear her grandmother's endless litany, Sajida took her to the terrace where she spent most of her time. It was a place with no one but crows and eagles. Though it was not easy to walk past her mother's tears and her sad eyes, it was her secret retreat – here, she could escape from the lewd curses that her grandmother uttered in her unbearably screechy voice. Here, she had learnt how to smell the different notes of the breeze and identify the colours in rain.

Looking at the broken chairs and the pieces of dead twigs scattered on the moss-covered floor of the terrace, Jessi asked, 'Hey, why have you brought me *here*?'

Saji was defiant, 'Because that's what I have decided. Did you come here to see me or to take a look at the house?'

'No, no. But it is very dirty here, it is not so easy to find a place to sit…' Jessima said as she deftly lifted the hem of her purdah off the ground and looked for a relatively clean surface.

Saji quickly pulled out a newspaper, tucked behind the water pipe to prevent it from flying away, and she spread it out. 'Sit here,' she said. Jessi was relieved and sat down cross-legged, exhaling 'Allahoo' as she did so, the paper crinkling gently underneath her.

For a while, both girls were unsure of what to discuss in this unfamiliar setting. Sajida's eyes were fixed on a hilltop in the distance and Jessima looked thoughtful.

'At least you are going to stay in a hostel, I'm being sent to the madrassa. They say that I can complete the Alima course in two years.'

'Yes, I'm going to the hostel. I will be gone in a week's time.' Sajida spoke as if she was a grown-up, a worldly woman.

'Well, you are also good in your studies. Look at me. Nothing gets inside my brain. That's why they are enrolling me in a madrassa.' Jessi was trying to blame herself to assuage her own sense of misfortune. Her long face and her thin body fidgeted, as if a strong gust of wind would be enough to sweep her off the terrace. She took Sajida's right hand and held it between her palms.

Sajida assumed Jessi was trying to console her and rejected the gesture of sympathy; she did not want anyone's pity. In fact, she was upset that her mother and grandmother had put her in this awkward situation in the first place.

'I have to leave in two days – ' she suddenly sounded

very enthusiastic. 'The school is very big, it's surrounded by loads of trees, and there's a playground, I loved everything about it.'

Jessi's face betrayed her weariness and envy. She realized that her sympathy and consolation were inconsequential to Sajida; she thought it pointless to stay here with her anymore. The evening breeze was very pleasant but at the same time she had to adjust her headscarf constantly. She had heard from her mother that talks were taking place about Saji's mother's remarriage. But Jessi did not have the guts to ask her friend about the matter, afraid that Saji might reply harshly; so she quietly got up in order to leave. Saji was silent, too, because she wanted Jessi to leave of her own free will.

Afterwards she stayed on the terrace watching the sky until it grew dark. Though it was difficult to avoid her father for fear of offending her mother and grandmother, she was also aware that if she had been living with him, she would have faced the same fate as Jessi – she would have had to go to the madrassa. *In a way this was better*, she decided, *much better*. She reminded herself of the proverb that everything good came with its own encumbrance. She started counting the days she had left in this house of tears. She felt sad knowing that her mother, unlike her, had no escape.

CHAPTER 13

The sound of goats bleating in the distance was pleasant to Mehar's ears and she listened indulgently in the backyard. Although the sultry heat struck her face, she was hesitant to go back inside the house. This was not worse than her mother's screams, she felt. The doubt that lingered in her mind – had she left Hasan in haste? – made her a little agitated. But after all, how could he have done something so cruel, when he knew her situation, when he knew her mother's situation – and how could she have put up with such an offence, she had to justify the events of her recent past to herself time and time again.

She was worried that her impulse to take revenge on Hasan, to show her anger towards him, had ended up turning her into a sacrificial goat. The portia tree in the backyard and the gourd creeper that was attempting to wrap itself around its trunk stood in as a memory of her life.

She thought of the time she had spent like a slave, like a dog, in Hasan's house. Had he ever let her do anything she liked? She could not remember a single instance where she had done something that he would have disapproved of. In a state of constant fear, she had developed a weakness of the bladder. Now, even though she wasn't sure where her next meal would come from, she was no longer afraid.

She wanted to travel back in time to live her life again – what would she have done differently? She wanted to have remained a child forever. This thought depressed her. After all, Sajida was but a child and yet her life already contained sorrow.

Mehar's heart ached when she thought how her daughter would go through difficulties in her later years without even the solace of wishing she could have stayed a child forever.

She resolved that Saji must not face the same path as her and that she must be educated. This was the only dream running through her head – she wanted it to be fulfilled and she wanted to stay alive so that she could watch it come true. She was aware that this would not happen quite so easily. This was the first time in a few months where she could spend a few minutes at peace, without listening to her mother's lamentations. Her mother's constant tears made her wonder if she had turned mad.

Yesterday, Saji had said, 'Nanni has become psycho, that's it!' Her actions seemed to suggest that perhaps there was some truth in that.

Every day, Mehar would be surprised by the extent to which it was possible to curse a man. For everything going wrong in her life, her mother seemed to blame Hasan. Asiya's helplessness caused this stress, and it made her speak in such a piteous manner; it was all merely a symptom of her utter powerlessness. Sometimes, she understood that in their society, this was the only freedom she really had. All the same, the prospect of living out the rest of her days listening to her mother's swears and oaths was quickly turning into a sorrow Mehar could not withstand. She had started to wonder if there would ever be any freedom from all this.

When Asiya had suggested that the two women consume poison and die together, Mehar was frightened. The fear that her mother could poison their food became unsettling – and she once again resumed thinking about a plan to escape from her mother's home.

CHAPTER 14

The street was ashen. The evening light was starting to descend along the backs of the homes and it made the scene strangely beautiful as children ran about, playing with cycle tyres. A horrible summer devoid of any rain had left its mark on the village. Women were hunched outside the threshold of their homes, gossiping about the neighbours in order to cope with their own stresses.

Parveen was looking out at the street from her window. These days, she was not in the mood to talk with anyone since no one was ready to give her the respect she wanted. Though even widows were offered sympathy as alms, she knew that a divorced woman was not worthy of such a basic level of identification, her pain was so shameful it could never be witnessed. Looking now at the children skittering across the street, the women busy with their chatter – all this appeared to soothe Parveen and knowing that, she immersed herself in being a spectator.

On the opposite side of the street, seven or eight women gathered in front of Abida's suddenly got up in a whirlwind and hurried inside the house. It was clear that they had spotted someone at the corner of the street. Parveen peered to see who it was. Rashid, Hasan and a few other young men were coming by to lead the Thursday preaching, having finished their afternoon prayers. They stood in front of each house for a few minutes at a time, repeating religious teachings before moving on to the next home. From behind a bolted window, she watched her brother's face closely. His face was not like before, he appeared tired.

Hasan lacked the vitality that had always defined his constitution, and even his eyes seemed dull. His beard was overgrown and grey. Parveen's eyes welled with tears and she felt struck by a deep sadness that he had lost his family because of his own foolishness. She could observe his hesitancy as he moved past her house and as he approached the house opposite.

'The Prophet (peace be upon him) said there is a gate in heaven called ar-Rayyan. On the Day of Judgement, only those who have kept the fast will enter Paradise through that gate. It shall be asked, "Who are all those that kept their fasts?" And upon hearing these words, they shall rise and none save them shall be able to enter through those gates. Once they have entered, those gates will be closed. So be afraid of the Lord.' Hasan's voice rang powerfully. As if they were eager for the men to leave, the women inside Abida's house came out and chorused, 'Allahoo,' as they sat down in the verandah.

Sitting at a height, Abida quickly scanned to see if Parveen was by the window and having confirmed to herself that she wasn't, she made a loud remark: 'The bridegroom just passed by, did you see?'

When Surayya did not understand who the butt of the joke was, Abida said, 'Of course! I'm referring to the bridegroom. He doesn't have the wherewithal to live with his wedded wife, he has abandoned her and is now preaching to the village about virtue. How shameless! And all the young men who are following him! I hope they do not follow his example and later say, "This is what Allah said, this is what the sharia says," they simply make up something so that they can marry again.' This was met by the resounding giggles of the women who had gathered around.

Such comments pricked Parveen but she felt sad, not angry.

Although it was true that they were mocking her brother, she did not feel that their criticism was wrong or misplaced. They were only saying the truth, she thought to herself. In the old days, when Hasan would come to the streets to preach, they would praise him, marvelling, 'At such a young age, he is filled with so much faith, so much ibaddat,' and today the same people were making fun of him. She knew that Hasan must be aware of this, and wondered how he was able to tolerate it all.

How must he feel living in the same village, on the very next street as his daughter, unable to even look at her? Parveen felt heartbroken and went inside her room to weep.

CHAPTER 15

Asiya's weeping started today with the sunrise. She never needed a specific reason to cry – she would start once she found the smallest excuse and then her tears would fall like dense rain.

Mehar was washing the agathi keerai in the kitchen. She had not yet started cooking, since she could only decide what to make after intuiting her mother's moods. Asiya's wailing had started early this morning.

'What could be so wrong so early in the morning, Allah! When will this end and when will I be able to cook!' Exasperated, Mehar leaned her back against a pillar. Ashraf had gone to see his father early this morning, too; he would eat something in the shop. She had to wake Sajida and make her eat, it was about time.

'What disregard and nerve that bastard must have to place his second wife in the front seat of his car, and drive around town before my very eyes. Let sand fall on his pride and honour.' Saying this, Asiya dropped the dirty pile of clothes that she held in her arms. The dust that rose from the dirty linen entered Mehar's eyes and she dropped the greens that she was holding to rub them. Tears were streaming down her face, and she wiped her cheeks quickly.

'What does it matter now? We have cast him away. We do not need him anymore. Who is he to us now? He is not my husband. He is not your son-in-law. Then why are you making such a fuss?' Mehar's voice was smarting.

'Oh, yes, you will say that he is not your husband or my son-in-law, but does he not have two children? Does he need all this pleasure and spectacle? Shouldn't he have done all this gallivanting in his youth, didn't he restrict you into staying at home while he remained separated from the children?' Asiya showered a slew of abuses on Hasan, while Mehar covered her ears, crossing her arms and twisting her face in disgust.

'Astaghfirullah, Astaghfirullah! You pray, you read the holy book – why do you use all these words!'

'That's how I will talk about him. I'm only speaking the truth – not a word of dishonesty passes my lips,' her mother retorted.

Asiya seemed to derive a great deal of happiness and pleasure from her words and speech, this much was apparent. After a small spell of silence, she stopped cursing and began lamenting again.

'Should he lead a life of happiness while my daughter who is not even thirty years of age must remain at home like a hermit?' Having asked the question, she also answered herself: 'I am going to marry you to Habibullah and give you a life that you never had with that bastard.'

Meharunnissa watched wide-eyed as her mother made this vow, wondering if she was speaking with a sound mind and conscience, or merely raving in her demented state.

She was afraid that her mother had indeed lost her mental balance. Her body appeared brittle and hunched, and her nerves and veins stood apart from her skin. For some reason, though, her face still retained its beauty. She must have been quite attractive in her younger days, Mehar thought.

'Hey, why are you looking at me like that? Do you think I've gone mad? I am perfectly sane. I won't die without seeing you live a good and happy life. I am going to make sure that you and Habi are married. You must live a full life right under that bastard's nose.' And so she swore, her words intermittently disrupted by her chronic cough. The tone of her voice was decisive, and that frightened Mehar.

The four walls of her tiny room which reeked of squalor, a kitchen full of lizards and cockroaches, her mother who kept cursing without pause: all of this pushed her into a depression. She was greatly afraid of the realization that this was to be her fate for the rest of her life, that a life she had not even anticipated in a nightmare was what awaited her. It felt like a punch to her gut.

The rest of her life? How long was that? Ten, twenty, thirty years: who knew except Allah!

These days, her mother's tantrums were becoming impossible to bear. In the middle of the night, she'd leave to wander the terrace to look up at the sky and curse Allah Himself. No one had any clue when her anger would subside. From time to time, the women of the neighbourhood came to Mehar and complained about Asiya's keening. *Hey Mehar, your mother is crying a lot, she is very tense, don't you see she could have a heart attack and die suddenly. And then you will be left an orphan. Why don't you advise her?*

As if her mother would listen to anything she had to say. Last night, Mehar had been reading the Quran, when her mother proposed that the entire family collectively commit suicide.

This was the third time she was hearing such words from her mother. Gathering all her strength, Mehar shouted: 'What is wrong with you Amma? You want my little innocent children to die in the years when they could most enjoy their life? Why should they pay for the sins of others?' The fear of what her mother's cruel mind might be capable of caused Mehar to stay awake all night.

Knowing that she was in for another sleepless night, she did the ritual ablution and started reading the Quran. But she was worried. She was enraged that the man who had entirely ruined her life could live happily without any feelings of guilt or remorse.

One day, when she had been married to him, she'd been watching a film. Unaware that he had returned home, she continued watching. He had approached, stood behind her and shouted. *You do not even realize I am home because you are admiring that man on the television! To look at another man and to lust after him is equivalent to becoming a prostitute – you know that, don't you?*

His voice had made her tremble in fear and she had felt humiliated.

And now, she could not forget the arrogance in his voice as he had said to her, on the day he had married another woman, *I am a man, I can have two wives,*

I can have four wives. I have the strength and the courage to do that. You are a woman, what can you do? Do whatever you can! This succession of thoughts interrupted her reading. She quickly closed the holy book and went to bed weeping bitterly. The urge to take revenge on Hasan sharpened.

CHAPTER 16

The entire house seemed to be awash with silence and emptiness. Since the children and Mehar had gone away the house had remained in this state of desolation, lacking life. Subaida could not bear it. Was all of this some kind of curse that had been placed on her family? Each insomniac night, she was invaded by this question. Her life had not been easy, and now, it was the same with her children. She grew vexed wondering if life held anything in store for her except tears and worries.

The visit of Hanifa Hazrat's wife the previous day had sent her into the throes of an even greater anxiety. 'Hey Subaida, I heard that Asiya is going to arrange the marriage of your daughter-in-law Mehar and Habibullah. What a test of our time this is! Just because a man does something, these women want to do it too.' After she left, the anger in Subaida's heart had yet to subside. She felt as though her brains were going to explode.

'A house like a palace, today it resembles a waste-land, with no children running around. If she too gets married, what will happen to the little ones?'

The way in which the wife of the Hazrat had delivered this news left no room for doubt about its veracity.

Subaida believed that someone had cast black magic on her family. She did not want even a second's delay – she wanted this witchcraft reversed as soon as possible. The thought of her son caused her to shiver imperceptibly. If he came to know about her suspicions, he would scream at her for being unreligious, he would kill her, even. He, too, was not visiting her these days.

She had told him clearly, 'Don't come here with that second wife of yours. I gave birth to you – I owe you something – so you may come and go, but don't bring that tramp here.'

Hasan had been defiant. 'Why? What did she ever do to you? Did she pull your hair, did she punch you? I married her – so shouldn't you be blaming me for how things have turned out?'

'Oh, yes! You will say these things! You are enjoying the pleasures of a new wife. But look at my house – look how empty it is with no children around—'

and Hasan had quickly and obstinately gone away.

Now, Subaida had a single objective: to remove the curse that had blackened her family home. There was no other way. She would have to make this journey without Hasan's knowledge, she decided, and wondered who she could take into her confidence. The only person who was knowledgeable about such things was Nafeesa.

Subaida comforted herself with the reasoning that to set right a family which had been torn apart it was not enough to merely make an entreaty to Allah. At the same time, she decided that it was important to ask Hanifa Hazrat to advise Mehar against marrying again. He would also have to impart this advice without making it appear that it came from Subaida otherwise it would craze Asiya even more.

'That foul-mouthed widow, that adamant devil,' she cursed her.

CHAPTER 17

Mehar wondered when she would be free of this hellish sadness, these hellish circumstances. She knew in her heart that her mother's cursing was merely a symptom of her helplessness, yet her constant grumbling suffocated Mehar, weighed her down, until she wanted to die. She thought deeply about how to escape her fate. No matter how things stood, she must leave this place at the earliest opportunity. On several days, the fear that her mother could have poisoned their food prevented her from eating, and she always made sure the children ate their meals under her supervision.

She did not understand how to escape from the clutches of someone who constantly came up with the idea of committing mass suicide as a family. Yesterday, when Parveen had visited her, she had shared her concerns with her former sister-in-law. But Parveen, too, didn't know how to handle this. She remarked dejectedly, 'You divorced him too hastily, Mehar.'

She had hardly finished her sentence when Mehar started shouting, 'How does that work? That man marries another woman and lives happily while I must keep going under the same roof like a servant?'

Mehar was still adamant that she had done the right thing. She believed that her righteous anger had not left her yet; still, she wished to exact greater revenge on Hasan. Parveen left. She, too, knew that she was not in a position to dispense advice on other people's problems.

Mehar's sole preoccupation was now escape. If marrying Habibullah was the only way out, she was looking for reasons she could justify such a decision and pacify herself to be open to the prospect. She reminded herself of all the humiliation and difficulty she had faced in her years of being married to Hasan. She would not have a better opportunity to take revenge on him. Not knowing how to escape her mother's incessant shouting and threats, she vacillated towards madness.

CHAPTER 18

These days, Sajida could not tolerate looking at her mother's blank and displaced expression; it made her afraid. In a few days she was going to go live in a hostel in town – and even as she happily anticipated this, she worried about leaving her mother behind. Ashraf ran in from the street carrying a torn kite. Tomorrow, his school would be starting. Since his school was only in the adjacent street, he could walk there himself.

'Hey Saji, give me some boiled rice. The tail of this kite is torn, I need to stick it up.' He touched her cheeks with his dirty hands as he begged her, but she only felt irritated by this.

'Do you only think of games all the time, you idiot?' she shouted, brushing the dirt off her cheeks.

'Please Di, I just asked Amma, but she won't even turn back to look at me, she's sitting like a stone,' he complained. He had lost considerable weight, his face looked tired. He lacked proper care, Saji thought, because he was going around on his own. 'All because our father married a second time,' she muttered to herself.

It was good that Asiya was not around; otherwise, even an offhanded remark like that would have set her off. Saji sighed deeply as she slowly walked to the kitchen. The vessels, the pots and pans, the dishware and utensils, all were in total disarray. A baby goat must have somehow made its way into the kitchen and wreaked havoc, leaving droppings everywhere. When Asiya returned home, she would surely scold her mother about this.

Saji quickly scooped out half a handful of cooked rice, gave it to Ashraf, then rolled up her sleeves and contemplated what needed doing in the kitchen. No one else on the street had a goat, so why did Asiya need one in the first place? She swept away the goat droppings and threw them in the bin. She wanted to remove all traces of disorder before her grandmother returned.

'What is all this—?' her grandmother's voice suddenly startled her – and completely taken in by the fear that her grandmother would start screaming, Sajida stared at her, silent and stunned. Asiya eyed her granddaughter with a critical perceptiveness, then hugged her gently and wept.

'Have you seen your mother? Have you seen how she is these days?'

Sajida could see up-close the sadness in Asiya's pinched face as tears streamed down her cheeks. Unsure of what to say, Sajida stared back at her without blinking.

'Haven't you seen that your mother is mentally disturbed? Ask her to get married, dear. If you say so, she will listen to you,' she said. 'I will look after you and your brother as if you are gold. My daughter never had a real life with your father. You ask her to get married.'

Sajida did not understand what her grandmother was saying. What was she trying to suggest? That her mother get married? When this woman made such a fuss when Aththa married again, and now she wanted Amma to do the same? Seeing her grandmother's pleading eyes, Sajida remained incapable of any reply.

CHAPTER 19

The incurable pain of having been cheated consumed Asiya. Mehar was married when she was fifteen years old; the groom lived in the next street and had appeared to be a good match so Asiya had got her daughter married without thinking twice. 'I do not want any dowry, as per the sharia I will pay the bride price and be married,' Hasan had said.

That horrible man had not let her daughter wrap even one of the exquisite saris that she had given to her as a wedding gift. There was no festivity, no cinema, no television. Leaving to attend a jamaat for female scholars for three months at some place or other, he would send her home. And even when Mehar visited her own mother in the next street, she would be covered head to toe, only her eyes visible through her burqa. She could not wear anklets like the other women in the village, nor even colourful clips in her hair.

Her daughter would rationalize it by saying, 'well, my husband does not like this' or 'what is the point of all this finery for someone who only stays at home?' On top of it all, she would slave away in the kitchen, making food for the jamaat and sending it to the mosque. And worse than everything, once in three months she ended up pregnant and came to her mother!

He does not want to use contraception. He says how can man prevent what Allah wills?

He had exploited Mehar's innocence to the hilt. Even today, she did not think that she had been cheated. She looked at life as a hardship that Allah was testing her through, and she cried accordingly. This was how Hasan had trained Mehar. Asiya was the one who could not bear it! She would spend her nights worrying about what would become of her daughter after death.

Habibullah did not have any children, and he would be with Mehar until the end without betraying her. She had asked him because there was no reason for him to say no to such an offer; he was a lovely man. But Asiya did not know what to do with Mehar. The first time she had broached the topic of remarriage, she had seen her daughter revolt and spew disgust.

Asiya had suffered her whole life without a male companion, so she knew the hardship of doing things single-handedly: bringing up children, taking them to school or – Allah forbid – the hospital, being in charge of a household and getting things done. She exemplified the human mind that looked for reasons to justify any decision.

CHAPTER 20

Sajida spoke with the gravitas of an older woman: 'You listen to Nanni, Amma. We will stay with her.' Mehar simply stared at her daughter with a blank expression.

Mehar herself was increasingly enraged with Hasan because of the state in which she found herself. It did not seem to matter to him that Mehar had asked for a divorce. Yesterday, even Sajida had cried to her about how he was going about town with his new wife in his car. She had seen it herself from the terrace. She grew angry when she thought how sad her daughter must have felt. She swore she would not let him remain in peace – and she kept thinking of other reasons to exact revenge on him.

Mehar knew that if she married Habibullah on her mother's advice it would torment Hasan and make him shrink in shame. She felt it would be a good way to hit back at him. But the thought of entering a marriage for this single reason made her stomach twist. Last night her mother had suggested, 'Come, let us all consume poison together' – and Mehar, broken and beaten, had finally replied, 'I will get married.' On hearing these words Asiya smiled as if she had forgotten all the difficulties life had cast her way.

It was enough for Mehar that her mother would no longer talk about her ritual group-suicide plan. She knew that she could not have continued like this forever, feeding her children in fear and remaining alert through the nights. It had become a major operation just to eat and sleep and wake up the next morning. She knew her mother's nature, all her grievances, all her slights and all the culprits responsible: the ones who had beaten her when she was just ten, the ones who had cheated her at twenty and the ones who had blamed her at forty – it was impossible for her to forgive or forget anything. Every day she would recollect each slight in some context or other and begin her cursing.

Like a cobra, she remembered each grievance clearly, all that she had endured in accumulation, and she waited to strike. Mehar herself wanted to prioritize two things: first, she wanted to escape from this suffocating and dark atmosphere where she was constantly hemmed in by her mother's complaints and litanies, and second, she wanted vengeance. These two circumstances led her to reach a decision that went beyond consideration of right or wrong. It was a decision guided by urgency and need.

—

Hanifa Hazrat had refused to go to Asiya's house to conduct the nikah. His wife, curious to hear the gossip, tried to make him go against his wishes: 'Please take a look at what is going on and come back and tell me about it!' But Hasan had shouted vociferously at him yesterday and he was afraid of what Hasan might do. He recommended Asiya call Hazrat Karim from the neighbouring village instead.

Sajida had gone to the hostel.

When the nikah was being performed, Asiya herself tied the black-beaded chain around her daughter's neck. Four people from the jamaat of the neighbouring village attended. The wedding took place without anyone else's knowledge. There was no festive lunch, no betel leaves, no garlands, no mehendi, no flowers, no fruits. It was like the marriage of dolls, or the pretend marriages Mehar would play at with her neighbour Abdul when they were children. They would play with toys and imaginary beads and made-up food, tying the thali, then making believe at house.

Now she felt she had been pushed back into child-hood. She was confused, unaware of what was going on. By the time the Hazrat read the marital decla-ration of shaheed she had completely slipped away, not responding until her mother pinched her thigh and told her to say salaam. As she came to her senses, responding with the correct address, even Mehar's voice sounded as though it was coming from the depths of a well. What else would life have in store for her, she wondered abstractly. She decided that she would see it all.

Mehar was wearing a new cotton sari. She had combed her hair after six long months, applied surma to her eyes and run jasmine oil through her hair. Even she could not identify or relate to what she saw in the mirror. She was seated in her room as if rooted to the spot. Was this really a doll's marriage?

Habibullah came from the next room, gave her his salaam and sat next to her. She returned his greetings and immediately said, 'I'm getting married only for my mother. Please do not assume otherwise.'

Hearing her bewildered voice, he replied, 'I know. That's good.'

—

Hasan behaved as if he had been completely disgraced.

'Does this female donkey have so much arrogance?' He could not contain his rage and fury.

'Why are you shouting in vain?' Hanifa Hazrat told him. 'When she asked for a divorce, you should have stopped it then and there. You should have pacified her. Now, she is not your wife, you and that girl are strangers to each other. There is nothing you can do.'

Like a wounded animal, Hasan was pushed into seeking retribution. He decided that henceforth Mehar would not be in charge of the children. Subaida had said to him, 'Now clasp your children firmly in your hands.'

And Hanifa Hazrat said, 'Your first wife has remarried, she cannot claim rights over the children according to sharia.'

CHAPTER 21

Sajida's hostel warden shouted, 'Saji, Saji.'

Her roommate Viji urged Sajida to rush. 'Come downstairs. Your father has come to meet you in the principal's room.'

Sajida was anxious. Why had Aththa come here? These were not even visitor's hours. What could be his excuse? Caught off guard, she took the dupatta she was wearing and wrapped it around like a head-scarf. The happiness of meeting her father after so long was mixed with the worry of not knowing how her mother would react to this.

Yet, the thought of standing in front of him only made her happy.

When she saw him in the office, his head bowed softly, tears sprang to her eyes. His beard was now rippled with white hair, longer than she ever remembered it being, and his white cap gently stirred under the fan. When she went and stood near him, he quickly raised his head and eagerly hugged his daughter. The yearning of many days could be felt in his embrace. As tears rolled down her cheeks, she began to weep – though she did not want to cry in front of her principal.

Sensing Saji's discomfort, and struck by the intimate familiarity of father and daughter, the principal gave Hasan permission to take Sajida out.

'You have to be back in two hours, no more, don't forget that.'

Hasan returned to his senses, somewhat overcome and discomfited, wiping his face with a handkerchief.

He and Saji walked out to his car. It had been so long since she had driven with him. She remembered the times when she and her brother and mother would travel in his car together. As she was about to get into the front passenger seat, her father's voice halted her: 'Go and get your burqa, my dear.'

Sajida realized that she was not wearing the burqa, and quickly walked back to cover herself. She was a little afraid when she thought how Aththa might react over the question of her education. Amma would take care of all that, she told herself. Besides, she was only studying in a girls' school, what was the problem with that?

The restaurant they went to was not very crowded.

It was another story during the weekends. She had been here a few times before the khula and before her mother was remarried.

Both of them were seated, not knowing what to say to each other. 'What are you going to have?' Hasan asked his daughter. But seeing her remain silent, he continued, pensive. 'Do you know how hard it is not to see you? And you did not even call me on the phone? What wrong did I do – don't you know how much I love you? Not being able to see you, to talk to you – I have suffered enough, my dear.'

She melted at the sight of tears welling up again in her father's eyes.

'It's not like that. I too cannot bear not to see you.' The little eyes behind her burqa were full of tears, secure in the faith that no one could see them.

After a long, long time, here she was, near her father and eating a tasty meal. It was almost as if the cursing female voices that had surrounded her in the last months had abated. She felt the peace of recovering her father's affection, the same father who had been cut out of her life. All the same, she was seized by the fear that he would put an end to her education and send her to a madrassa. This was an inevitable fear. And then another thought: she must hide the fact of her father's visit from her mother and grandmother.

When her father did not make any negative remarks about her studies, Sajida was surprised. He, too, was careful not to say or do anything that could upset her. She knew that this was the result of her mother's actions and she was happy. Even when she was a little girl, Aththa had always scolded her: *Don't wear skirts... cover your face... don't wear anklets* – and she felt confident now that he would not be able to control her the way he used to.

He was happy merely to see his daughter who had been denied the chance to speak with him.

But though the long-enduring battle of wills between Saji and her father had come to a resolution, the thought that he loved another woman – more than all of them – made her feel an excruciating jealousy. That was unacceptable.

That night, she dreamt she was travelling with her father in his car. She smiled to herself with the realization that neither her mother nor the new wife were there.

CHAPTER 22

Three days ago, Hasan had sent word via Hanifa Hazrat's wife: 'From now onwards, only I will take care of Sajida, I am her wali, she has no rights at this point. If this Habi goes to the hostel to fetch my girl, I will cut his feet. When I – the father – am here, he shouldn't be the one going to collect my daughter.'

After Sajida had left for the hostel, the house itself had transformed. These days, Ashraf was hardly to be found at home either – he spent all his time with his father, and it was enough for him to be around his toys and his father's car. Moreover, he hated when his grandmother, angry that he had gone to see his father, would shout at him when he did return. Two days ago, when she had scolded him again, he clapped both his hands to his ears and ran away crying, 'Oh no, my ears are paining,' and had not returned since.

Mehar was like a lifeless object. She did not know what she could do to abate her mother's cries.

Habibullah had gone away to somewhere in Kerala for his job. Like a little cricket, he mostly kept himself to himself. She had gone and stayed at his place for a week – she had gone there because it was unbearable to be here, with her mother. He organized his day in such a manner that it appeared she did not even inhabit the same space. Once, the maidservant Sabiramma had whispered to her, 'He is not a good man, that is why he went so long without getting married.' Her tone seemed to be full of sympathy towards Mehar, but Mehar felt nothing; neither curious nor eager to know about any of the things the other woman had to say, so Sabiramma's sympathy did not find much use.

It was a mistake to have assumed that her mother's lamentations would soon come to an end once Mehar remarried. Any reason was sufficient grounds for Asiya to begin shouting her protestations. Seemingly, her grief was related to Sajida's absence.

He has sent word that Saji is his child. So much concern for his child, isn't that why he got married again without informing anyone?

At least when the children were around, Mehar could carry on with her daily life without having to pay heed to what her mother was saying. Their needs would occupy her attention, and deflect from Asiya's

misery. Now they were not there. Seeing Ashraf running wild on the streets, she called out to him through
the window. It had been three days since she'd cooked
for him, fed him with her own hands; now she didn't
know if he was even eating properly. She felt shaken
by this thought.

It was only after her new marriage that Ashraf had
stopped coming by, and Saji had not returned from the
hostel even once – from now on, only Hasan would
collect her and drop her back. Perhaps she had made
a mistake in listening to her mother and remarrying.
Mehar grew afraid that Hasan would say something to
the children and try to separate them from her.

She consoled herself that no matter what, a daughter would always understand her mother. Then she
thought how her children might not have enough to
eat at her mother's place, how they had grown thinner
as a result of not eating under her own watchful eye.
This depressed her. She, too, was only half her former
self. Nowadays she avoided looking at her shrunken
body, avoided mirrors altogether. She would often
wonder – is this face the same one that used to look
so beautiful?

Everything had passed her by. What was the point
of thinking about such things, she reasoned.

Nowadays, not one of the women from the

neighbouring homes visited her. In fact, they no longer seemed to consider the existence of this family in their midst – perhaps this was one of the reasons for her mother's constant raving. In the old days, the wife of Hazrat Hanifa and the women of the house opposite would spend so much time here, enjoying the spectacle of setting her mother on edge with their snide remarks: *Hasan should not have married for the second time. He has ruined the life of your daughter, this innocent young woman.* Mehar would want to prevent them from visiting, but she would never explicitly say so, afraid of hurting her mother. Not perceiving their true intentions, her mother foolishly believed these women were full of real compassion for her.

Now after Mehar's second marriage, these women had stopped visiting Asiya's home – and neither did she go to theirs. A few times, Mehar had tried to goad Asiya. 'Why do you remain shut inside this house like me – why don't you go and sit in the verandah for a little while, enjoy the breeze?' to which her mother would respond, 'Oh! Leave it!'

On hearing the knock on the door, Mehar was jolted from her chain of thoughts, surprised that some-one might be paying a call. Her mother pretended not to hear anything and sat stubbornly with her back to the wall. Mehar rose from her chair, walked past her mother, and opened the door. It was Parveen.

Parveen's face appeared as dry as a crumpled ball of paper. Wrapped in her own grief, Mehar had believed that only she could be so broken – but seeing Parveen she was indeed shocked. She was perspiring slightly, which made her appear much older than her years, and her body was as thin as a broomstick under her heavy purdah. The knowledge that their lives seemed to be heading on a similar course softened Mehar. 'Come sit, Parveen,' she said kindly.

Asiya greeted Parveen with a nod. She was still seated against the wall, her demeanour like one who was gravely ill. Parveen removed her purdah, and sat close to Asiya. She enquired about her health. Mehar could observe – merely in the manner in which Parveen removed her purdah – that she was frustrated and upset.

Asiya began crying as though something had finally managed to slice through all her bolted sorrow. The anger that she had suppressed within found an outlet. The three of them, sitting together in that house, gave the impression of being worn-out figures – not one of them in any position to console the other. It seemed like an insurmountable task just to look for words of comfort.

A long silence found its place in their midst,

representing the muteness of broken hearts. They looked at one another, wondering who should break the silence first. Afraid that allowing Asiya to begin would end in a long lamentation, Parveen spoke up and tore through the heavy stillness in the air.

'Why did you marry again? Did you lose your mind?' Her sharp voice was piercing.

Asiya responded like a wounded animal: 'Oh, so you are here to support your brother! Oh, yes, of course – now I understand!' The helplessness that lurked behind her cruel tone was enough to shake Parveen, but she pretended not to be affected.

'You cannot hold your tongue for even a little while. I am asking Mehar.' Parveen realized that her words came out a little cruder than she had intended. So she, too, was capable of so much harshness and anger, she thought sadly.

Her loud voice appeared to explode on Mehar and Asiya's faces, their features slowly absorbing the impact of Parveen's words. Mehar was unable even to discern whether her former sister-in-law's words were motivated by anger, concern or sympathy.

Life sometimes brings with it snatches where one does not realize the time or the day – and the women were pushing towards just that sort of faltering state. Mehar sat for a long time, silent, shocked. She did not know how to answer Parveen, what tone to take. Nor did she know what to say. She was overwhelmed.

Why *did* she marry again? To save her mother from her lamentations? To escape the very walls of this house, these walls that shed endless, countless tears? To believe she could lead a life that she had been denied? Or, more than any of this, to seek vengeance?

Mehar – unable to articulate or explain her actions – hugged Parveen and started to cry. Her tears conveyed guilt, and she sought penance in Parveen's embrace, aware that her doing so might incite her mother's rage.

Asiya refused to accept this as her failure, refused to see how her pure intentions to try to set something right had backfired. She knew that if she accepted her own failings, she would come across to Mehar as someone who had wrecked her life.

Then Mehar felt as if she had cried enough. What was the point of crying now? Would her eyes ever dry up? Had they not cried enough these long six months? She did not know what to make of the unknown challenges that lay ahead. She did not know what would come of Sajida's studies. She could not understand if Hasan would allow Ashraf to visit her. How was she to spend her years without her children? She was suddenly frightened that she had provided

Hasan with an opportunity to seek retribution against her. She felt as though her head would burst from the pressure of all these thoughts.

Parveen started slowly, 'It seems Hasan visited Sajida at her school yesterday. Amma said that he was planning to enrol Ashraf in some boarding school in another town.' Parveen's voice was full of anxiety. Mehar could see that Parveen, too, wanted to unload her sorrow.

Hasan knew that Mehar was inseparable from her children. He knew that if Ashraf missed a single meal, she would be perplexed and look for him in absolute panic. Parveen did not want to tell Mehar what Hasan had said to their mother: of his plans to remove Mehar's immoral influence from the children. According to Islamic law, Mehar did not have any rights to her own children. This was what he had told Amma.

Mehar was shocked. 'Is he going to send Ashraf to a hostel? He is just a baby!' Her tone betrayed her disbelief. But the experience of having lived with Hasan made her realize that he was capable of doing anything. Such a fact could not be expressed verbally – it was simply something Mehar had learnt herself, through past experience.

'Is he going to punish my innocent children under

the guise of separating them from me?' Mehar started screaming and sobbing.

Parveen felt as if she was being submerged in the midst of all this relentless crying. Asiya sat motionless with a blank expression. Parveen wondered what Asiya was thinking, how she had been stunned into total silence for once. Unsure of what would happen now, Parveen wiped her own tears and started making a move towards her home.

Darkness had fallen. Parveen felt a pang of guilt when she realized she had forgotten her prayers in the midst of all this drama.

CHAPTER 23

When Ashraf threw a tantrum, it made Hasan extremely angry – he slapped him hard on his face a couple of times. His anger did not subside. 'Son of a runaway bitch,' he said. Ashraf was crying from the pain. Subaida sat nearby and watched all of this unfold with a sorrowful expression.

Although she knew that there was nothing she could do to control her son, she softly said, 'He is only a small child. He wants to be playful, it is that age. Let him be if he does not go to pray. When he is old enough, he will offer prayers on his own. Every little kid goes to the cinema – and he might have just gone because of his friends. Let it go!'

He cut her short with his angry words. 'Leave me to this and remain silent. When I am trying to teach him ibaddat and strengthen his faith, why do you allow shaitaan to roam freely in this house?' He once again resumed beating Ashraf. 'Will you go to the cinema again? Will you come to the mosque on time for the prayers?'

Ashraf panted, 'no Aththa, now I will not go to the cinema.' His cheeks streamed with hot tears. Hasan knocked him on the head again. 'Will you visit her house again?' It was a forceful rap. 'No, Aththa, I won't, I won't go again,' Ashraf screamed again and he fell to the floor, reeling from the pain.

'In one week, I am going to have you nailed to a hostel,' Hasan said. He left the house and walked towards the mosque.

It was shameful that nobody in the village respected him. Every day after the early morning subuh prayers, he would go to each street and write the hadith of the day on the blackboards that were placed there. In the mornings, men in groups of four would be taking their walk towards the lakeside – and because they found his work beneficial, they would stop by and give him their greetings. Now, he had a feeling that they hesitated to talk to him. The day he had married again, things had changed irrevocably. But this treatment had worsened only after he was served notice of divorce by Mehar and she had remarried.

He grumbled that it had taken a woman to reduce his respect and social standing. He was enraged and decided that he must not let her be at peace with her decision to remarry. Just because a man did something, why would a woman be allowed to do the same? The thought made his blood boil.

He had been a little heartened by having met Sajida after such a long time and more so by how she had spoken to him, like in the old days. Having completed his ablutions, he started his prayer. He reasoned that Mehar had made all these mistakes because she was not brought up in the proper manner. 'Show my children the right path and feed them strength in their faith, Allah,' he prayed as his lifted his hands. He planned to bring Sajida to his side gradually by teaching her the right things. In this regard, he was willing to raise his two hands in prayer and ask Allah for His help for as many days as it would take.

He was very sad that Mehar had now cursed her children – they would always be known as the children of the runaway woman. Seized by such raging thoughts, he was unable to pray with a present heart and mind. He felt as if the devil had come and sat behind him and was distracting him from communicating directly with God Himself. Hasan tried to concentrate. One question still bothered him: was society trying to tell him indirectly that what he'd done – believing it to be the right thing – was actually wrong?

CHAPTER 24

Parveen felt that she had to help Mehar, somehow. But she did not know how! She asked her mother, 'Poor Ashraf – he is still such a small boy. Why must he be sent to a hostel? How do you feel about the matter?' Subaida replied, 'But who can even talk to Hasan. I cannot.'

Lying in bed, Parveen looked through the window, out at the street, thinking how her life was just a series of empty memories. Like a sari that had not been pleated properly, the street was full of irregular folds of little verandahs, a trademark of Muslim streets, spilling onto the width of the road. She had seen the Hindu streets a little distance away. Almost as if there was an invisible line marking the symmetry, they would be neat and long, the houses clearly defined. She thought this was perhaps because Hindu women did not have the necessity to sit someplace outdoors to talk among themselves, as Muslim women did.

She thought of her mother's plan to visit a witch doctor to lift the black magic which had been cast on their family. Like a mango materializing out of thin air, she thought, and wondered how lifting the curse would solve all the problems faced by their family overnight. *Even Allah would not know how to release us from all these troubles*, she pondered.

She heard Nanni cough. Her life was better off than most. Because she could not see, she had not married, had not been forced to move away, and she did not have any children. It was a peaceful life, one she had created for herself, one that revolved around sustenance: food and prayer. It was also a fitting surprise that even in her old age she did not suffer from any disease or ailment. Was it possible that anyone these days was not on some sort of medication? Her own mother's meals were dominated by a myriad of tablets and tinctures – Parveen thought that this was perhaps a blessing that had been uniquely bestowed on Nanni.

No one had any peace in their life. Why? Was it because of ignorance? Was that the only reason? Parveen felt as though her head would explode.

CHAPTER 25

When a young man came one afternoon to Hanifa Hazrat's home with the message that he was being summoned by the jamaat leader, Amjad, he was surprised. He didn't have the faintest clue as to why Amjad bhai would want to meet him. Wondering what this was all about, he slipped back into his tunic.

His wife expressed her surprise too when she saw him getting dressed. 'You just changed your clothes and said you were going to sleep,' she said to him. He patiently replied, 'It seems Amjad bhai wants to meet me, he has sent word, so I will go and find out more once I meet him.' He wore his prayer cap and headed out. 'Do lock the door, you do not want the goat coming inside the house and pissing here,' he instructed.

Although he only lived on the next street, it was infuriating to have to walk in the midday sun. 'Why does this old man have to be summoned at this cruel hour?' he grumbled to himself. The heat was unbearable and there was no sign of life on the streets.

What could this be about? Was Amjad going to ask him about the kandhuri festival? He could not surmise a reason, and this left him baffled.

Amjad's home was three storeys high and impressive. Hanifa Hazrat took his first steps into the verandah timidly. Amjad opened the door and greeted him with a 'salaam alaykum' and Hanifa returned his greeting and followed him inside. Amjad was only wearing his baniyan, this was clearly the time for a post-lunch nap. What could be so pressing and urgent?

Amjad asked him to sit on a sofa and he sat facing him. Hazrat Hanifa sat with a little hesitation, a little trepidatious of sitting on such an expensive sofa. He tried, discreetly, to gauge the economic prosperity of this household. Amjad was not interested in beating around the bush. He was very direct.

'Hey, what is all this business concerning this Hasan? I heard his wife has not only given divorce but that she has remarried now.'

Hanifa Hazrat looked at him with surprise, as if it was unusual for the leader of a jamaat to find out about this sort of thing so late in the day. 'Yes, this all took place two weeks ago,' he said.

'What do I know about this sort of nonsense. I

was away on business and I just returned to the village,' Amjad said, a little gruffly. 'If such things happen don't you think the reputation of our village will be ruined? How could you elders merely be bystanders of such a deed? Men are prone to stepping out of bounds. He can marry four women, fine. If women do the same, don't you think this will become habitual. What is all this uncultured behaviour?'

Amjad hit his palm against his bald head. His face had already been red with anger, but now it shone even more vividly like a ripe tomato.

Hanifa replied tentatively, 'What can we do about it? Asiya was very adamant. When I asked her, she said to me that Islam allows for women to marry a second time. I said I would not be attending. For the nikah ceremony, they invited the Hazrat from the next village.' Hanifa Hazrat was suddenly very relieved that he himself had not gone to the wedding ceremony. His tiny whisper was hardly audible even to himself. He wondered whether Amjad heard any of his explanations. A little louder now, he continued: 'Moreover, that is a part of what our sharia laws say – what can be said against it?' He tried to explain his own helplessness in order to make Amjad understand.

'For that reason, should we allow women to do everything that the law lets them do? Every rule has its exceptions, Hazrat,' he said. 'Now if a couple of other women follow this trend, what will come of the honour of our families, our small village? Will others not make fun of our jamaat, and will they not say that the leader of the jamaat is useless?' Amjad bhai's voice quivered with a mixture of extreme anger and extreme helplessness. His fury made him wheeze.

'That pussy-chasing, emasculated Hasan – was he just watching all this? It would be better if he had slapped her and strangled her to death!'

Hanifa understood that Amjad was talking boldly, but that his bark was worse than his bite. When Amjad's voice reached such a decibel, a woman's head peeked out of the kitchen and quickly went back in. Both men observed this, and there was a shift in the room.

'If there is anything further, I will call you,' Amjad said firmly, indirectly asking Hanifa Hazrat to leave.

Hanifa Hazrat got up from the sofa clumsily and repeated his salaams.

'This man wants to be leader of the jamaat, and he is keeping this position merely for the sake of his prestige,' he grumbled to himself as he headed home. He cursed Amjad. 'In this boiling heat, he is making an aged man like me go to his house to hear him spout nonsense!' He pushed open the door to his own house forcefully.

If people like Amjad were leaders of a jamaat, this was how things would go wrong, he thought to himself morosely. There was no sign of his wife, so he assumed she must be napping. He praised Allah, feeling calmer now, removed his tunic and placed it on the hanger. Then he drank a glass of cold water which had been placed on his bedside table. He stroked his beard and closed his eyes. He remembered Mehar as a small child, indeed she had grown up in front of his own eyes. He thought of everything that had happened, all of it, Hasan's second marriage, the khula, Mehar's remarriage. He could not say what was right and what was wrong, all he could say was that everything seemed to have taken place in haste, clumsily, thoughtlessly. Although it was true that the problem started because of Hasan's folly, Asiya's desire to settle scores had been a mistake. He did not know whom to blame at this point. For his part, he had sent his wife a couple of times to Asiya's to give them good counsel.

One evening, she had said to him: 'If you send me again to Asiya's house and ask me to talk to her, you will see the other side of me. I'm warning you. She looks at me as if I'm going to her place to beg for alms, or something. "Don't keep coming here," she says, "I've only now managed to convince my daughter

to get married – you will sway her with your unso-
licited nonsense and change her mind." Let whatever
happens happen. I have a feeling that if this marriage
doesn't go through, they may commit group suicide.'

Shocked by his wife's words, Hanifa Hazrat had
stopped asking her to talk to the women. *Let this go
the way Allah wills it*, he had said to himself.

'When did you come back?' Sulaiamma asked as
she entered the room, breaking him out of his mus-
ings. Her face betrayed her curiosity about what had
happened at the jamaat leader's house. Then she felt a
pang of pity and said, 'You sleep a little, I will also rest
my eyes.' She sat down at the edge of the bed. Seeing
her face full of questions, the Hazrat thought of an
adirasam swollen with frying oil.

'How can I sleep when I think of that poor Mehar
child's life…' he sighed.

In an effort to allow him to get it all off his chest,
Sulaiamma just stared at the bedspread, nodding.

'Amjad is indeed behaving unfairly. He is blaming
me for not preventing all of this from happening in
our village. Everything about Mehar's marriage – the
law allows it. If they choose to go ahead and do it,
what is in our hands?'

There was a tone of resignation in his voice that
touched Sulaiamma too. Nowadays hardly anyone

kept up any sort of affiliation with Asiya's family. The women spoke ill of both Asiya and Mehar, as if their immoral influence was a source of contagion, and not condemning it unequivocally would reflect badly on them. Even Sulaiammaa had heard the things they were saying.

'Amjad is questioning me now. But would this have come to pass if he had scolded Hasan for coming back with this new wife? Or if he had chased her far away? Would this have come to pass if Mehar had been prevented from giving divorce? What is the point of seeking justice now? On top of everything, this sort of man is the leader of our jamaat, and our village?'

His voice showed genuine concern and affection even as it was underscored by utter helplessness. 'Everything is His doing,' Sulaiamma said and she lay down next to him. The hot air being circulated by the ceiling fan spread over their bodies.

CHAPTER 26

Subaida said that she was going somewhere today – without Hasan's knowledge – to get the curse removed. An uncle, Subaida's mother's sibling, Amina's younger brother, lived there. 'He himself is very good at removing black magic and through him I will meet someone else.'

Parveen replied gravely, 'If only your son learns about this, he will kill you.'

It's true that Subaida was afraid of her son, but she was furious at him too. It was because of his actions that all this ruin had come about: this is what Subaida thought to herself, but she said nothing.

Parveen was looking out of the window. The sky was suffused with yellow, and somewhere in the distance, two birds were chasing each other; it was very beautiful to look at the scene. Such moments brought to light ripples of longing. Both the sky and its colour reminded Parveen that the body does not always hide its needs. She tried to distract herself from this mindset.

It was not a very difficult task. It had become part of her routine, and she controlled herself and tried to channel her thoughts to other things. So, she now thought of Sikander Uncle, the younger brother of Amina Nanni.

She must have been about ten years old. One day, the entire household had been thrown into a frenzy. She'd just returned home from school.

Her mother said, 'My Uncle Sikander is coming. Go wear some beautiful clothes. Wash your face and put on some powder.' Her face was overflowing with happiness. It was very rare to see her mother like this. Although Parveen caught her mother's contagious smile, she did not understand what the fanfare was about. Her Nanni sat majestically on the bed wearing a new sari, a ring on each finger, her neck decked with heavy jewellery. The smell of various sweets and savouries from the kitchen filled the house. Hasan had bought bags of fruit and put them in the hall.

She went to Nanni, and asked her softly, 'Who is this Sikander uncle, Nanni?' Nanni was happy to have her nearby, she made her sit by her side. 'It is my younger brother – when he was about fifteen he suddenly ran away. Where he went, why he went, for what he went, no one knew. Some said that he had gone to Pakistan. Others would report having seen him here or there – but there was no word from him. For thirty-five years, until yesterday, we knew nothing!

'There was no prayer when we did not think of him. Today Allah has granted our prayers. He is coming from the Andamans it seems. I'm unfortunate to be blind – I will not even know how he looks.' She sighed.

If there was anything Parveen had to know, she asked Nanni. She would answer her questions. No one spoke much to Nanni, so she had developed a knack of speaking to those who respected her enough to seek her out. Nanni was everything. Often, she did not have all the answers to Parveen's questions. She never thought to exaggerate her stories with the sole purpose of making Parveen happy, but to a stranger observing their interactions, it would appear as though Nanni's only objective was to delight the little girl. Seeing them talk to each other, hearing the tall tales that Nanni would churn out for her, Hasan and her mother would listen with amused smiles.

Nanni would lose her cool if she detected anyone mocking her. She would shout to no end, that's how angry she would become. Seeing her mother shiver in the presence of her Nanni would make Parveen burst into laughter. Nothing that Nanni said her mother liked, but unable to say anything openly, she would simply mutter something to herself. As a child, Parveen secretly enjoyed this tension between the two women.

Parveen was curious. A guest was coming home from the Andamans. What were the Andamans? Was it a big place, was that why her mother was so excited? What would the guest look like? What dress would he be wearing? She was imagining all of this. Of course, he would be wearing shirts and trousers like Kamal and Rajni – just as in the films, she'd thought. To all her questions Nanni gave clear answers. Because the guest was coming from a foreign country, he would have landed in Chennai in a plane. It was not clear what he'd be getting them. Parveen had asked Hasan who said, 'When Jafar Uncle came from Singapore, he got us foreign pens and foreign chocolate. Uncle Sikander, too, will also get us something, wait and see.'

After that, she could not wait even a single second. She did not want to appear like a villager in front of someone visiting from abroad. So she went inside and wore the blouse and skirt that she had got for Ramzan. She tried jumping up and down facing the little mirror in the bathroom to see if she could see her full figure. She scrubbed her face with Lux soap until it almost disappeared behind foamy suds, then rinsed and dried, then applied powder. She combed her hair and put it in a ponytail. Her mother was very busy as the hour of Sikander's arrival neared. She had made a plate ready for the arati. When Parveen went to her and asked, 'Amma, can I take the arati of the guest?', Subaida told her that only she would do it. Parveen felt very disappointed. If she was the first to welcome the visitor from abroad by taking the arati, only then would he pay any attention to her. To hide her disappointment, she moved a little away, but whatever thoughts ran through her mind, her innocent face would betray her. Her mother would immediately ask her, 'Why are you keeping a long face? You already have big lips, now they are literally hanging off your face. Don't sulk!'

Parveen remembered how she had been warned that such pouts would ruin her beauty, so she had consciously softened her facial features.

The visitor came home after the azar prayers were finished. He offered his prayers at the mosque and came home right away. Her mother was at the entrance of their house, taking the arati, so she quickly ran to stand shyly at her mother's legs, clutching her sari. She observed the visitor. He was a tall man, he wore a kurta-pyjama. Most of his face was hidden by his thick black and white beard. He was only carrying a small bag, probably not containing any gifts. His beard reminded Parveen of the beard of the ghost who appeared in the film *Pattanathil Bhootham*.

The man said salaam to her mother, clasping both her hands. Then he entered the house, sat near Nanni and greeted her. Parveen's face darkened with disappointment. She felt cheated because she was expecting a handsome man to appear in modern clothes. Her desire to be near him faded, so she went to a corner and stood near a pillar. It was like looking at the Hazrat. She wondered how someone who looked like this could have spent time abroad. A little while later, the visitor pointed at her and asked, 'Who is this, Subaida?'

Her mother answered, 'This is my daughter, Parveen.' He stretched both his hands towards her and asked her to come near. She approached him halfheartedly. When she was close, he kept his hands on her head and said, 'Alhamdulillah.' The smell of attar that came from him was overpowering, so she sauntered quickly into another room while the adults tittered.

For two days there were several special banquets

in Sikander's honour. He narrated all his stories to Amina Nanni and to Subaida. He explained in great detail how he went to Andaman, and how he spent his days in Chennai.

Only one piece of information held interest for her. It seems he had cured a lot of people with his magic. When the famous actor Asokan's son could not walk, he had healed him. Sikandar explained that in real life Asokan was not like the characters he portrayed in the movies, that he was quite charming.

That information alone seemed sufficient to her. She had told everyone at school that her relative knew the actor Asokan very well and that he had visited him at his home, embellishing details of Asokan's glamorous home.

Today her mother had gone in search of this Sikander. Parveen sighed. Now it was her opportunity to avoid dashing her mother's deluded hopes. She did not want to contest Amma's beliefs.

CHAPTER 27

Ashraf went to the hostel. Mehar was not told about the fact, but she knew that Hasan would have prevented her son from telling her about this. She understood that Hasan's way of getting back at her was to separate the children from her – but she didn't know how to live without them. To whom could she go, from where could she seek justice?

Her eyes and her throat had dried up from all the crying. No one was willing to listen to her cries or screams. Parveen had said to her, 'Who will talk with that fool? He will not listen.' She understood that nobody could stop Hasan at this point.

Her mother had once again started her lamentations. It felt as if she had come to a place of unending sorrow. Only one thing was clear: without her children, the very children she had birthed, she could not see even a grain of happiness in her future.

The fear that perhaps she had committed a

grievous mistake still scared her. How to live away from the children? Although Saji sometimes called her on the phone now and then, it was the absence of Ashraf that seemed to be irreplaceable. Even today, he did not know to eat by himself or take a shower on his own. Both Saji and Ashraf had been so tiny when they'd been born, the doctor had told her that her children had weak constitutions. She remembered that he'd scolded Asiya for having married her off at such a young age.

Will my days pass in regretting what I have lost, she thought to herself and began looking for her burqa.

For the last six months, she had stayed indoors, not setting foot outside except for the one week she spent at Habibullah's place. Not knowing where her burqa had disappeared to she grasped quickly for her mother's scarf. She took it off the clothes line, wrapped it around herself and started towards Hanifa Hazrat's house. She had left home without even her mother's knowledge, listening to Asiya mutter to herself in her room as she quietly closed the door behind her.

It was comforting to see that there was nobody on the streets at nine o'clock at night. There was no moon in the sky, and even the streetlights were not working. It was as if they recognized Mehar's embarrassment at being seen, protecting her under cover of darkness.

Once she was at Hanifa Hazrat's house, she knocked at the door timidly, afraid of attracting attention from the neighbours. A dog limped past. The atmosphere was stifling. She heard Sulaiamma ask, 'Who's there?' and softly replied, 'Please let me in, it's me.' She hesitated to say her own name, as if it was a bad curse. As she opened the door, Sulaiamma crinkled her old curious eyes and asked, 'Mehar, is that you?' to which she replied, 'Yes, it's me.'

'Is Uncle here? May I speak to him?' Mehar asked upon entering the verandah of the house, still hesitant and cautious. Sulaiamma called to her husband and spread out a mat for Mehar to sit down on. When Hanifa Hazrat emerged from indoors, he stood for a moment in silence, looking at Mehar pensively. 'What brings you here child, at this hour?' he asked.

Her scrawny frame was sufficient to rouse his sympathy. So long he had imagined her disturbed state based on Sulaiamma's descriptions alone. Today, on encountering her in person, he saw how badly she was faring.

'He has taken my son and enrolled him somewhere. He even prevents him from talking to me. Please ask him to give my child back to me. I birthed him, my belly aches with sadness, he is but a baby.' She rocked as she cried violently.

Sulaiamma, angered by this injustice, cursed Hasan, 'To separate the child from Mehar, that devil has put the child in a hostel and ruined his health!'

'Calm yourself, Sulaiamma. When this girl married again, he felt spited. According to our law, the child belongs to the father, he is their custodian – what can we say? If anyone approaches him, he will quote a thousand laws, hadiths and sharia codes...' Hazrat's speech gave away his helplessness, it was evident he had spent some time thinking over the matter. Mehar presented herself as the picture of a beggar, her hands outstretched, eyes filled with thick tears. She felt as if her dreams and her sleep had been snatched away. Now this was like a punch to her gut.

Perhaps there was indeed no one who could retrieve her child – and the thought made her weep mercilessly. She stuffed the end of her sari as a seal against her mouth but still she continued to wail. Her tears would have crushed the hearts of anyone who heard them.

Hazrat Hanifa asked her to pray to Allah to intercede and tried to comfort her with words of the Holy Book. Sulaiamma, not knowing what to do, merely sat in silence. The darkness which had occupied a corner of the verandah now settled on Mehar's face.

It was a frightful sight. Mehar sat there, not knowing how to take leave. Sulaiamma stared blankly, considering how to tactfully send her back home. Like a dangerous well, her presence spread panic.

CHAPTER 28

Parveen was waiting for her mother to return. She had left early in the morning, and was not yet back. Parveen did not know what she was up to. She was not fearful on her mother's behalf because she knew Subaida had taken someone along for company. Her mother had all the diseases one could possibly have at her age: diabetes, high blood pressure, kidney trouble – so she never travelled alone anywhere. 'Where is she going to go? What's beyond the village anyway?' she muttered to herself.

She was greatly concerned about Ashraf. He had come to see her before he left for boarding school. His eyes were swollen with too much crying. 'I do not want to go. Can't you tell my father, Kuppi?' he cried to her. She hugged him and she too shed tears. He was tiny, skin and bones, and his body trembled like a little leaf. Parveen felt a visceral hatred for her brother when she thought of how he was fulfilling his plan to strike back at Mehar by making his own child scream in such a manner. Who could talk sense to him? Allah alone, it seemed.

Parveen merely caressed the child's back, turning over her violent thoughts. His puny body did not reveal his true age. Mehar never left her children alone for a minute. This little boy was a fussy eater, and Mehar would feed him every mouthful because he refused to eat by himself. Parveen would reprimand her: *don't feed him, serve the food on his plate, he has to learn to eat by himself.* Her sister-in-law would pay no heed.

Parveen could not bear her brother's intention to send this little child to a faraway hostel for the sole purpose of separating him from Mehar. But try as she might, she had no clue what to do. She tried now to give the child the necessary courage to face his future. Hearing her granddaughter struggle to console the little boy, Nanni said, 'Call up that ruined man. I will spit on him.'

Nanni was angry, and it surprised Parveen to see the old woman capable of so much anger after such a long time. She slowly whispered, 'Please tell your mother before you leave,' to which the boy said, 'No, Aththa will beat me, he has asked me not to go there, he beats me for going there.'

Seeing this little child come up with a list of complaints, Parveen felt as if her heart itself would burst. 'It is only for a little time,' she managed to say, 'read well and come back here.' She stroked his hair and kissed him goodbye.

Her head reeled as she sat with her back against the wall awaiting her mother's return. When Amma finally came, it felt like a silent tune was playing in her head. Subaida placed the bag in her hand near the grindstone in the corner, removed her headscarf and hung it on the clothes line. She wiped her face with the end of her sari, all without saying a single word. She went into the toilet and shut the door. Parveen watched her, nervous. Normally her mother's activities would take place with a flutter – observing her taciturn behaviour, Parveen concluded that there was bad news. That was the only possibility.

Parveen waited patiently. Her mother was washing herself for the prayers. Parveen sat, watching her mother's actions closely. She felt that her manner had changed... Normally her mother would have a spring in her step, a strut, almost, that belied her age. Or perhaps it was something to hide her age. Today, all that was gone. She even pursed her lips in a way that suggested that she did not want to say anything.

'Why don't you say something? What did Sikander

maama say? Did you eat, can I make you tea?' Parveen asked her question after question, expecting that there would be some answer, some clue to be revealed.

'No need. We've done some rituals to get rid of the bad stuff. I'll tell you later.' She went on to offer her prayers.

For some reason, Parveen was worried and stressed by her mother's increased silence. She started walking towards Nanni's home – with the hope that tomorrow her mother would tell her more. Outside, the hot air in the street struck her cheeks violently.

CHAPTER 29

It had been two months now since Mehar had even heard Ashraf's voice. She felt sure she would go mad. Her head throbbed day and night. She had already taken three Saridon tablets this afternoon – but the medicine did not help her much, it only caused stomach ulcers. Since she had also not eaten, her pain was more aggravated. Sulaiamma said to her, 'Sajida is a big girl, she has come of age. Do not send Habibullah to fetch her. It seems Hasan will handle that.'

These days Hasan would visit his daughter at the hostel twice a month. Once, when he brought her home for the holidays, he put her up at his mother Subaida's house. Without his knowledge, and with Subaida's permission, Sajida came to visit Mehar in secret. Mehar burst into tears when she saw her child. Saji had changed so much in her appearance; she was thinner, darker, her skin full of mosquito bite scars, her hair entangled and lice-ridden. It took a long time for Mehar to stop crying.

For some reason, Sajida was peculiarly reserved. Like a bird talking to itself, she was seated on her own. Like someone who did not understand that bird's language, Mehar struggled. Even as her face revealed her anxiety about her daughter's silence, she stared at her intently.

Asiya's voice – as usual – clanged on with its complaints. 'That ruined man is separating the children from my daughter and torturing her. Allah, will you not hear me?' Saying so, she unscrewed a bottle of oil, applied some on Sajida's hair and started undoing her plaits.

'Are you eating? Are you starving? You've become so thin, my poor child!' Tears streamed down her face even as she started combing her granddaughter's hair.

Mehar finally understood something. She could see from her daughter's sharp looks and gestures that her children hated her. Her innocent daughter's face appeared to have darkened, her oval face was even thinner and longer.

Mehar felt that the things Hasan had probably told their daughter was reflected in her thoughts and actions. She felt depressed. She wondered if it was real, or if she was imagining that her daughter's eyes contained great confusion and never-ending sorrow.

'Did you speak to your brother?' she asked in the softest voice.

'Hmm. Yes, we spoke. It seems he is doing good. He cries now and then, but it is better now. He will stay there.' Saji carried her voice like a poised woman now. Mehar asked in her broken, overeager speech, now louder, 'Is he eating properly? Has he become thinner? Is he better?'

'I don't know. It's not like I saw him, no? I'm just repeating what Aththa said, it seems he is not eating properly.'

Sajida was wearing a very expensive chudidhar dress and good-quality slippers; a beautiful watch glimmered on her wrist. It seemed Hasan was spoiling her with material things. In her heart, Mehar knew that she had made a mistake by depriving her children of their father's love for more than six months. But still, at least now, it seemed both father and daughter had re-established their relationship. If Hasan had been separated from his daughter, it would only have made things more convenient and joyful for his second wife, Mehar thought bitterly.

But, Mehar wondered, what if Hasan had said something to Sajida that could alienate her from her own mother? For the first time, she could feel in Saji's manner a certain distance, a cold reserve. This was against her daughter's nature, was it not?

'Oh no! Look, how much hair is falling out! Don't you comb and wash your hair?' Asiya asked her grand-daughter with concern. Then, she took the lice comb, spread a white towel on her lap and started cleaning her Saji's hair with great tenderness. Sajida remained oblivious to what was going on around her. There was indeed great difference in her behaviour, her face and her impassive liquid eyes.

Mehar keenly observed Sajida's eyes as they made note of each detail of the house. Immediately grasping her intention, Mehar said quickly, 'Habi has gone to Kerala for business.' But suddenly, before she could finish the sentence, she felt ashamed, her body recoiling involuntarily. Although she remained silent, Asiya was racked with guilt seeing her daughter shrink with shame in her own daughter's presence. For the first time, she realized what a great distress she had caused in her daughter's life, in her granddaughter's life, even. She was shocked – how sadly mistaken she had been in assuming that she had created an alternate life for her girls...

Sajida saw her mother's sunken cheeks and her hollow eyes and lowered her gaze. The black beads around her mother's neck, which symbolized her marriage to Habibullah, annoyed her.

I made a mistake. I left my wife and children and got married. What did your mother do? She left her children and got married. Is that right? The words of her father rang in her ears. Her heart was filled with hatred. This evening, her old schoolmates would visit, knowing that Saji was back. She did not know how to face them. Suddenly, she wanted to leave.

Night was slowly descending even as these thoughts dispersed and diffused through the minds of the three women.

The look of absolute remorse on her mother's face made Mehar unbearably sad. She did not want her mother to feel responsible for everything that had happened. She knew that any sense of guilt would only push her to endless grief, and she was determined not to cause her any more sorrow when she was living only for Mehar's sake. It was true that her mother's insistence, her pleading threats and pressure had pushed Mehar towards the decision to marry. But hadn't Mehar also wanted to make Hasan pay for his cruelty and thoughtlessness? Hadn't she wanted to humiliate and belittle him? She could not deny her own role in all this. Neither could she brush away her desire to escape her mother's tears.

The food that she had lovingly prepared for Saijda – khulcha rice and meat kurma – grew cold.

CHAPTER 30

Parveen wiped away the beads of sweat on her face with the ends of her sari, then held the fabric to her mouth. She tried to arouse herself by touching her breasts and her intimate parts. Her thighs clasped together tightly and the heat that rose between them made her huff rapidly, short breaths in and out, the pleasure burning – and when she eventually climaxed, she let out a long sigh. Her body was wet but she felt incredibly light. She had no idea for how many long years she would have to pleasure herself like this. She felt that she had to grow old like Nanni to move past this vulgarity. Perhaps Nanni knew the pain of this sadness better than her. At least Parveen had been intimate with a man in her life, but there had been nothing like that in Nanni's life.

Rahim would do everything, and at some point, when he would still not be able to get an erection, he would feel extremely ashamed. Once, when he failed despite trying repeatedly, he grew tired and turned to face away from her. Seeing that he was distraught and upset, she put her arm around his back. To offer support, she said soothingly, 'Don't worry, we can talk to the doctor.' Her words flung him into rage. 'Shut your mouth. Why don't you invite the whole village for a feast and share this news?'

She never understood why he got so angry. She had not said anything with malice; there was simply a problem and she had suggested going to the doctor. What was so wrong with that? And how could someone who had been kissing her and holding her, saying so many words of love just a few moments ago, turn to such violent fury so easily?

She had wondered if he was afraid that she would not respect him for his impotence or if she would tell others when an opportunity arose.

Later, having tried again with her on a few other occasions, he grew distant and left her altogether.

Was it justified that her life had been ruined because of someone else's failing, a failing which happened for whatever reason? Surely, Rahim would not have married her if he had known about his condition. He would not have had any sexual experience before his marriage. If he had, why would he subject himself to humiliation one more time? On the other hand, perhaps he knew of it, but agreed to this marriage owing to pressure from his parents. Whatever the reason, her life had come to an end.

She felt it was better to be alone in this manner instead of becoming someone's second wife and bringing up his children. It was enough to make love to herself once in a while, when the nights became unbearable.

Nanni had taught her about avoiding certain types of food that could increase her libido and make her torment worse.

She heard the neighbour's dogs barking. She wondered who was out on the streets at midnight causing the dogs to bark. It must be someone returning from the cinema. Through the window she saw her neighbour Salam return home. She knew that he desired her; when his wife wasn't around, he would try to make a pass at Parveen. For that reason alone, she pretended not to notice him. With many such confusing thoughts, she tried to sleep now.

CHAPTER 31

Hasan had been angry all morning, not knowing what
to do with his anger nor how to bring it under control. Sabi, from the small grocery shop by the mosque,
had taunted him, 'What machchaan, you preach all
this only for the village? You speak of ibaddat, sharia,
hadith, and nothing applies to you?' Hasan had felt
revolted.

He was making fun of Hasan because, according to
him, Hasan's mother had gone somewhere to reverse
some black magic cast on her family. But it was more
than that. Each of his words hid one thousand meanings. Hasan felt as though he was being mocked for
the fact that his ex-wife had married again.

Once, when Hasan had seen Sabi's sister idly
chatting with Kaja at night, he planned for days to
catch them red-handed; he had scolded the pair and
had taken the matter up with Faisal at the mosque.
Surely this had caused Sabi to rail against him now,

not willing to give up a good opportunity to mock Hasan.

'He's preaching to the village, but his mother believes in black magic and he is not able to stop her.' Sabi expressed his mockery with his crude gestures and intonation. A few people were drinking tea at a shop nearby. His voice gave away his attempt to catch their attention. A dog on the street paused to stare at the scene.

Not knowing if this charge against his mother was true or false, Hasan contemplated the possibility for a moment. Rage overtook him, he lurched forward to throw a punch. 'Who said so? Can you prove it?'

'Hmm. Who else went with your mother but my aunt? First go and ask her, and then come to me.' Sabi pushed Hasan away and got on with his work, hanging bottles of Coke and Pepsi and bananas on the façade of his shop.

'Hey, what did you say, scum? If this turns out to be false, I'm going to slash your throat,' Hasan threatened the shopkeeper, seething. He started his TVS-50 engine and pushed home. He was shaken. Could it be true? If it was just gossip, the guy would've been afraid to affirm something so serious... He felt nervous, a chill ran through him, as though his very body was resigned to the truth of Sabi's statement. *Why would*

Amma behave this way? Already the entire village knows about my business, and now this, now where can we hide these blemishes? He stopped outside his home, sombre, then went inside with great resolve. When he saw that his mother was offering prayers, he stood silently in a corner, leaning against the door.

She greeted him, 'Salaam alaykum, what is the matter son?' 'Nothing, finish your prayers,' he said. The anger in his face made her insides churn. 'I've finished now,' she said – and added, 'come and sit,' as she gestured towards the sofa.

'Did you go somewhere to get some black magic removed?' His question was direct, clipped. What she had dreaded was now unravelling quickly. For a few moments, she stared into space, not knowing what to say. 'Yes, I went – just like that – you see—' Every word was broken.

'Kafir. Why do you even bother to pray? You have found equals to Allah, what is the need for you to pray. Shaitaan. Shaitaan!' His shouting was cruel.

'Dogs who were once afraid to even stand in front of me are now challenging me, they are pushing me on the street—' He was overtaken with humiliation. He felt as if all the respect and honour he had once commanded had evaporated into thin air. He took his left hand to draw out his beard, and even as his fingers quivered in torment, he desperately sought some pretence at control. 'I preach the hadith to the whole village and ask people to stay away from the shaitaan. But it seems I've been doing that in vain when the iblis in my own house is committing shirk and blasphemy.'

Subaida, afraid that the neighbours would hear Hasan's diatribe, went to close the windows and the entrance door. 'For what are you closing the doors,' said Hasan, his voice like a wild scream. 'The whole world is laughing at us. Go and see what the word on the streets is.'

It appeared as if he was deliberately raising his voice to make himself heard by the outside world, for others to know that he was the type of man who could chastise his own mother. She felt that if it had been someone other than her, he might even have beaten them up. Seeing the cruelty behind his anger, Subaida said vindictively, 'Yes, I went. Since birth, I have been facing untold hardship. There is not a single day when I don't pray, but that Allah seems to be beating down my family again and again, I somehow wanted something good to happen, so I went. What problem is it of yours?' her voice lashed.

In a corner of her heart, she felt a small hope that her emotional outburst might melt away his anger.

'Go, then!' Hasan retorted. 'Go to temple after temple and ask those gods. You asked Allah and it did not happen, so why not ask other gods. What a fool you are! You lack intelligence! Can one ascribe other equals to Allah – no, everything is gone. All the goodness, prayers, faith – everything is gone – you are going to hell.'

His voice grew louder. At first, Subaida had felt that her neighbours should not hear anything, that that would be improper, but now she wished they would hear the manner in which her own son was shouting at her. She earnestly desired for the village to learn that she had gone to a sorcerer against the wishes of her son, and that still, he had firmly held to his righteous views. After all, only then could he continue preaching to everyone – he could attend his tablighi jamaat and continue his life as before. Otherwise, the village would mock him, and he would be incapacitated with shame. Being a mother, this was her perspective.

'Allah has said that life on this earth is not life. What matters is the afterlife, the life we live in heaven. This life is not important. "I will give all kinds of sorrows and tests to my people in their earthly life; the one who retains faith through all of it, only he can reach heaven" – this is what Allah says. All these

sorrows, these are his tests for you – please understand." He finished his long sermon, his facial features
relaxing a little. Subaida was concerned to see him
with his voice trembling, his reddened face, his body
covered in sweat. How could it be that so many people in this world were so happy, she thought to herself.
She sat silently.

Perhaps Mehar had left Hasan because she was
unable to bear this attitude of his. Yet as soon as this
thought floated in Subaida's mind, she pinned it down
to unravel its meaning carefully.

There were no special days. She could not do the
fatiha, she should not leave the house. She should not
watch movies, she should not stand in the street, and
if and when she did step out, if she absolutely had to,
even her eyes should not be visible under the burqa.
She should not wear lipstick, she should not wear
jewellery, she should not watch TV, she should not
go to the dargah with the neighbouring ladies, she
should not use contraceptives, she should not abort
her foetus. Subaida exhaled, 'Allahoo.'

'I went, what has happened has happened. What
do you expect me to do now?' she asked calmly, as if
there was no problem at all.

'My shame and honour have turned to dust,'
Hasan replied. 'Who will listen to me now? They will

instead tell me to go and preach to my mother.'

Subaida replied calmly, 'If anyone says something like that, tell that guy to come to me, I will give a fitting reply. I will tell each of them to look at the flood in their own cunts.'

Unable to tolerate his mother speaking so coarsely and knowing that it wasn't going to help things if he stayed any longer, Hasan hastily got away. When the sound of his engine faded away, Subaida thought to herself: *Shame and respect? Does he really still think there is anything left?*

She started reading the Quran. It was enough for her to get peace by any means necessary. She did not want anyone telling her what was forbidden and what was permissible. Even as she muttered all this, she read in a meditative manner.

CHAPTER 32

Amina took the jug of water from her bedside – slowly feeling its curved handle with her fingers, cupping its base in her other hand with utmost care. She said bismillah and drank the water.

The village was at a standstill, lacking in any excitement. It had been almost seventy years since she had learnt to discern whether it was day or night, light or dark, feeling her way through sounds and emotions. She sighed. How long could this go on? She had not lost a single tooth, nor even a strand of her hair, and when Parveen had once remarked that it was not even all grey, she had felt proud. Now she felt that there was no point to any of it.

She still believed that she could grasp what was going on around her through sense and memory. Hearing the sound of a goat trotting along the street outside her window, she was capable of noting that it was limping on one foot. She was so perceptive that merely listening to a passer-by's walk, she could intuit which of her neighbours it was. And so, in the case of someone like Parveen who was also leading a life similar to hers, she could interpret each breath through her own memories, refer back to the meanings she had stored in her own dictionary. It gave her great sorrow to realize that her granddaughter was now suffering the same insurmountable struggle she had faced fifty years ago.

In her time, it was not such a problem. She was blind. It was enough that she stayed in her corner and ate what was fed to her. But Parveen's time was not like that. There was TV and books and cinema… Amina worried how Parveen negotiated all that.

When she was young, Amina had struggled a great deal on sleepless nights when the desire arose to touch herself, and she worried that someone might catch her in the act. When she bathed in a toilet that lacked a door, with only jute bags as a screen, she would touch her own breasts under the cover of applying soap. She would long for her own body with unquenchable thirst; she would imagine how it would be if this body was given to a man. Afraid that somebody would enter if they did not hear the sound of pouring water, she would constantly splash loudly as she washed herself. One day, while she was bathing, she heard someone enter suddenly. She was shocked when she was kissed on the lips and then, clasped; for a few minutes, her body was subject to a man's brutal hands.

Just as swiftly as it had come, the figure disappeared. Amina was transfixed with happiness. She wondered who the mysterious figure might have been, even as she took pleasure from that shocking embrace. Was it Murugan who came to deliver milk, was it Palani the gardener, or her neighbour Aziz? She could not quite describe the rawness of it all. From the coarseness of the hands, she concluded that they must belong to a peasant. She asked her mother for the names of everyone who had visited the house that day, but her answers did not lead her to a satisfactory solution, and she never did find out who the stranger was.

Whoever those hands belonged to, she wanted them to embrace her again. She waited for it. Every time she took a bath, she would wait a little for those hands. That body, which ran away in fear, never came back again. For the remainder of her life, she had to provide comfort by herself.

She only lacked sight. Although her body was otherwise perfectly functional, no one came forward to marry her. She pitied Parveen, and wondered why her own fate had also befallen this younger woman in her family. She consoled herself, thinking that perhaps this was a better fate than being a man's slave.

On a few nights, the sounds of Parveen's sighs and the restless rolling on her bed would also leave Amina sleepless.

CHAPTER 33

'If she stays here all the time she will go mad thinking of the children. Let me take her to Kerala. Send her with me – some change will do her good.'

Habi's request seemed right to Asiya. If Mehar went away for six months, she would possibly forget her sorrows. At the same time, she was afraid to broach the idea to her teary-eyed daughter.

'Why don't you ask her, I'm afraid,' she told Habi.

'Me? No, you ask her yourself,' he replied, retreating quickly.

Asiya was afraid that if Mehar continued in this state of obsession, she would turn mad. She herself wept that her own actions would perhaps lead to her daughter losing her mind.

Habi looked at his mother-in-law, contemplating how things stood. He wondered why Asiya was always crying and cursing, and he thought that it was possible she suffered from mental problems. Whenever he saw her she was always in such a state.

Habibullah's aunt Fatima had told him, 'That Asiya is a loosu. If Mehar stays with her, she will lose her mental balance, you must take her away.'

Mehar was even thinner than before. There was no life in her large blank eyes. Habibullah felt pity for her. He had not been greatly interested in the marriage, but had agreed to it because he felt that it would somehow be helpful – but it had only made things worse. Hasan took the children away and his cruel actions had now driven Mehar to such a state. Even Habi was afraid of Hasan, and feared that if he got a chance, he'd beat him up.

Asiya went and sat next to Mehar and stroked her hair, 'My dear, why don't you go with Habi to Kerala for some time. Maybe six months or so. In the meanwhile, we can arbitrate about the children and have them back. What are you going to do by staying here and crying all the time?' Mehar silently turned towards her mother. Every day with her mother was pushing her further towards hellish distress. Perhaps this was Allah's way of separating the two.

But she did not like that it was Habibullah she had to go away with, and she worried what Sajida and Ashraf would think of this. On the other hand, Mehar also did not know how to while away her

time here. It was almost as if they had been ostracized – no one in the village spoke to either her or
Asiya, nor did they visit their home. The entire village seemed to have developed some sort of hatred
towards Asiyamma. Some thought her mad; others
that her thirst for competition, her uncouth need to
insist that her daughter could do exactly what a man
could do, had come back to bite her in the ass; others,
still, that her bad fortune was contagious.

Every day at least two women of Mehar's age
would come along from somewhere, whispering
loudly to each other, to provoke her. *How does she
manage without her children? She's never been separated
from them even for a day!*

But it wasn't just she who was suffering, Mehar
knew. Her mother, too, remained indoors all the
time. She was not attending any wedding ceremonies or special occasions in other people's homes....
She realized that they had lost the social standing to
talk to others. She burst into tears, bewildered, as she
weighed her options – considering how her children
would react and how her mother would handle life
all alone.

Asiya tried to ease her daughter's concerns, saying,
'You go, and when Sajida is coming home for her
holidays, you come back. And with Ashraf too.'

There was no way to prevent the neighbours from their malicious gossip mongering, so Asiya decided that she had to do everything possible to send her daughter away with Habi. She called Sajida at school and told her that since Ashraf had gone away, Mehar's health had deteriorated – she told her that Habi had asked her if he could take Mehar to Kerala for treatment.

Sajida broke into tears on the phone. She wanted to talk to her mother. 'Don't worry, my dear heart,' Asiya replied, cutting the phone call short, 'when mother's well, she will return, next week she will talk to you.'

———

Mehar's travel to Kerala also took place as per her mother's decisions. Habi had a small shop where he sold ready-made clothes in Kannur. In the apartment building where he stayed, the Malayali women were all educated. They went to work, drove scooters and cars, wore jeans and t-shirts, and spoke only in English. They had a variety of hairstyles. Everything was new to Mehar. For the first time in her life she stepped out on the streets without wearing a burqa. Habi took her shopping. They went to the cinema. He told his neighbours Rosie and Girija to take her with them if they were going outside.

For Mehar, it was fascinating just to observe these women. Seeing them glide about independently made her yearn for the same freedom. It was also comforting to realize that people here did not spend their time monitoring others – and there was so much peace in the knowledge that no one knew anything about her.

Only then did she realize what Hasan's ibaddat had really meant. Perhaps if Mehar had been born in a town, she too would have led a life like these women. Because they spoke in English among themselves, she couldn't talk with them. And because of an inferiority complex, she was afraid to even stand in their presence.

Habibullah was a perfectly fine husband and theirs was a perfectly fine arrangement; Mehar was glad that she had told him not to touch her, and he had taken some of her jewellery to operate his small business. And yet, every night she wept because she was separated from her children.

Both Sajida and she would cry when they were on the phone. They promised to meet during Saji's vacations. Whenever Mehar cooked for Habi, she lamented that she was making food for a stranger while letting her own children starve.

This house in Kerala too was drenched with her

tears. At first, she had compared her life with those of the women around her. Later, she felt fervently that her daughter must be able to lead a life like the educated women around her.

Not a single night passed without tears, and even Habi's patience was worn out. Once, he said a little roughly: 'If you loved your children so much, why did you get married?' She had calmly replied, 'I wanted to hurt him.'

After that, he never asked her any questions – he was not ready to hear such answers.

CHAPTER 34

Hasan was driving like a madman as they approached the village. Sajida was sick with typhoid fever, and the car journey made her feel even sicker. They had seen the doctor, they were not returning home, despite the fact that she had wanted to rest for a week before going back to the hostel. As she had left suddenly, she had been unable to inform either her mother or grandmother. She could not call them while her father was around, and had thought to herself that she would talk to them once she was back at the village.

Now her whole body was under extreme pain. Instead of nourishing her, hostel food had dried her up. After all the tests at the hospital and chats with the doctors, she felt even more tired. At a time like this she longed to be with her mother. But her father's brutal nature could never understand that a sick child would want to be with their mother. When they had lived together, her mother had to struggle so much against him, even to fulfil the smallest of their wishes. She thought about that often.

Aththa would kill her if she mentioned she wanted to be with Amma. *From morning to noon, I'm the one who is taking you to the hospital, looking after you, and you want to be with that runaway woman.* Even thinking of the words that he would use and the tone in which he would say these things was excruciating. She tried to close her eyes and rest with her head turned to the window.

'Do you know where that runaway is in Kerala with her husband?'

His cruel, taunting voice blocked her ears. Sleep was not possible. When he started cursing her mother he would not stop, and she knew she would have to keep listening to this till they reached home. Forlorn, she looked out at the oncoming traffic.

When she lived with her mother she had to hear bitter curses and complaints about her father. When she was with him, she had to listen to all his shouting about her mother. These days, she was happiest not seeing either of them. Although her hostel food was measly and without flavour, and the accommodation lacking in comfort, she felt a relief when she got to stay there even when the girls were allowed two days' leave.

In the beginning, she had thought that Ashraf was happy with things, always joking around – but one day, he confessed, 'I cannot be with either of them. They are cursing or lamenting all the time, it's so irritating.'

She thought how her little brother hadn't wanted to go away to a hostel. But their father had been adamant, he had to go.

Once Ashraf told her, 'Those two have made mistakes but we are the ones being punished and sent away. Mental.'

Even she had been a little pained. How long would this state of affairs continue? There seemed to be no end in sight. She didn't hear any of her father's ramblings – she was so lost in her own thoughts… It was a good thing she was sitting in the back seat. For Hasan's part, he was not bothered if she was listening or not, and he continued to shout, even though she had now switched on her headset under her burqa.

She knew what he'd say: *no point respecting your mother, don't talk to her, she left her children on the streets.* She was tired of hearing it constantly. She wondered if there was nothing else for him to talk about with his children, curious to know what other parents in other families spoke about with their children. She made a note to ask Jessi and Shubnum while she was in the village.

The heat grew more intense as they neared the village, and Saji saw the roadside convent school that signalled they were there. It was where she had once gone to school – a beautiful place surrounded by hills and trees and large fields. She loved seeing it.

He stopped the car in front of her grandmother Subaida's home and asked her to get down. She felt very tired, and struggled with the effort. He took her bag and fruits out, placed them by her feet, and said to her, 'Remember to take your medicines promptly.' Then he drove away. Sajida could not understand what had got into him, why wasn't he coming inside the house? She entered, lethargic and weary. Subaida Nanni was lying down on the bed, her belly a small hilltop rising and lowering with her breathing. On seeing Saji, she sat up and tied her hair.

'Salaam Nanni,' Sajida said. 'I came with Aththa, why did he not come inside?' she asked. She removed her burqa and lay down next to the old woman. Subaida did not say anything. Hasan had not come again since he had shouted at her the other day. She had not called him, preferring to wait for his anger to subside.

She had comforted herself. After all, she had simply done what she had wanted to, she had not set out to hurt him or anyone else. And yet she was gnawed by the feeling that what she had done ran counter to the spirit of her son's religious work, all his good intentions to do right and show others the right path… It had been a mistake. Now nobody in the village would respect him and she felt responsible for his situation.

Subaida sighed. She wanted to forget this. She held Sajida and gently touched her forehead. 'There is no fever now,' she said softly. She felt great pity on seeing Sajida's slight frame. 'A girl who has come of age must be strong and eat well,' she chided lovingly. She took Sajida's bag and placed it in her room.

Viji had already come in the morning to sweep the room and clean it up. Now Subaida spread a fresh sheet over the bed and took Sajida inside so she could rest.

'What can I do but blame Allah for all this ruin,' she sighed, trying still to justify her visit to the sorcerer in this manner. Suddenly angered, she even cursed Hasan's second wife and Asiya and Mehar, they were all stupid bitches. There was no use in scolding anyone. She seemed to realize it, and yet she could not internalize it. She cursed these women long into the night.

CHAPTER 35

'What's your name, chechi?' Girija asked Mehar. 'Meharunnissa,' she replied. She was piling the ready-made clothes neatly one on top of the other in the living room.

Girija was seated on the sofa. She asked, 'What have you studied? Why don't you go for a job?' Mehar only half understood her question because of the language barrier. 'Oh,' she answered, 'sixth standard,' and signed the number with both her hands. She felt shame course through her body as she realized that others would consider this pretty inadequate.

'Oh ok, so you are a housewife,' Girija laughed. 'Chechi, you must come to our house,' Girija said, also explicating this in her gestures. Mehar nodded as if she understood.

Girija was wearing a shirt and a blouse. She was Mehar's age. But her clothes and her make-up, her face free of worry, made her look much younger.

Whenever Mehar looked at her own face after see-ing Girija, she would be struck by how much she had aged, and she mourned the loss of her beauty. Her face clearly gave away the fact that she was a villager. But she was not in a situation where she could spend time worrying about it. What was the point? Her life had passed her by. What more could she worry about? Ashraf's face danced in front of her eyes.

During the children's school holidays, she had gone back to the village so that she could see them. Only Sajida had visited her. Ashraf refused to come even though he was also staying at Subaida's place, and even though Sajida had pointedly asked him.

Every evening that holiday, Mehar would wait by the door when he was cycling out on the streets. Seeing him in the distance, she would step out and stop his cycle when it approached her house. He would wriggle awkwardly, fearful that his father would find out and scold him.

'Please come home to Amma,' she would beg, hugging him, pulling him close. 'No, no. I'll come later' he'd refuse adamantly and speed off on his cycle. Mehar would feel ashamed, then, because the entire street would gawk at the scene, and she would return indoors away from the judgemental eyes of the other women. Seeing her cry, Saji said, 'Leave him, Ma. He is too scared of Aththa.'

Mehar felt her stomach burn. Another two months to go till the children's annual exams. How would she remain alive until then? It had been so long since she had spoken to her mother or Saji on the phone. The phone bills were mounting – this was Kerala, after all, and there were roaming charges, so Habi would only let her speak for a few minutes once a week.

His income and expenditure were the same as back at home.

From time to time, when they were free, Girija and Rosie would come and chat in the balcony. Mehar lived in the last apartment of the block, and they lived in the fourth and the fifth flats. From far away, she would look at them through her window, and it was impossible to not feel jealous of Rosie's modern clothes, her bob cut and her fluent English. Perhaps because they were Christians they got to wear clothes that exposed their thighs.

I should have been born in Kerala, Muslim women here can at least study, such sad thoughts would run through Mehar's mind. Then she would chasten herself for thinking such things when she was facing more urgent calamities.

At times, it seemed to her that everyone else in this world was at peace. She saw them laugh, wearing good clothes, watching TV. She would compare her situation with theirs, and invariably cry more and exaggerate the nature of her troubles. *I too am a woman like them… But why do I alone have such a bad life?* The reasons for her stubborn comparisons kept growing.

She regretted that she had cried when Hasan had left her, assuming that her life had ended. Why had she not thought to get just such an independent life, like the women around her now? Like a child being exposed to the outside world for the first time, she was trying to grasp large truths, asking questions and interacting with the world around her with wide-eyed wonder. She realized that her life with Hasan had been nothing to mourn, and her tears had been in vain. She realized that the second marriage that she entered into, with the motive of taking revenge on Hasan, was stupid. She was tortured by her own devastating thoughts and she hated herself. Nothing would compensate for the sorrow of being separated from her children.

In this manner, she was lost in thought. She observed the street through the window. It was twilight now. She could see a tree with its spread-out branches, and a tea shop on the side street. A few men were seated here and there on benches in the tea shop, in veshti, in baniyans, large moustaches. Even worse than the men in her village, she thought, not wanting to look at them any longer.

There was a sudden gust of wind which threw up garbage from the street. A piece of paper flew quite high and reminded her of Ashraf's kites. She remembered that she had to cook something. Again, the thought of cooking for someone while she couldn't make food for her own children made her upset. She also remembered that it was prayer time.

CHAPTER 36

After months of persuasion from her family friend and neighbour Nafeesa, Parveen took the first steps towards her own independence. She and Nafeesa opened up an account in the local bank, enrolling themselves as the president and secretary of a self-help group. Now they could do something. And Parveen did not want to stay home forever.

One day the two women went into town to meet the Block Development Officer. Parveen knew Vanaja, who was the official in charge of social welfare. The building was right next to the district collector's office. As they stood outside in the scorching sun, waiting to be called in, the time spent in waiting was sufficient for Parveen to dig out old memories. Rahim had taken her one day to her mother's house with the idea that he would come again the following week to pick her up. But he never came back. She called him many times, he did not pick up the phone.

Neither did his parents. She had been worried, so she went with her mother to find out more.

The front and back entrance to the house was locked. When they rang the doorbell, Parveen saw someone furtively open a front-facing window and close it abruptly. They stood there without under-standing anything.

It was about five in the evening. They had left home after eating lunch, and had opted to come in a taxi, carrying heavy boxes of freshly made murukku, with the intention that Subaida would return later on her own. Parveen could see the women in nearby homes peeking out of their windows. Confused, she once again pressed the doorbell, but there was no response.

At a distance, they saw a female police officer on a motorcycle. She and her mother exchanged con-fused glances. The woman police constable came up to them and said, 'You cannot go inside. Leave, leave.' Parveen was enraged. She shouted, 'This is my house, who are you to chase me away?' Parveen could feel the eyes of the whole street upon her, and Subaida was on the verge of tears, unable to comprehend what was going on. Her body was shaking, heart sinking.

'Only your father-in-law sent me, ma. He said there was some problem. he said that you could come back after talking it through.' Everything became clear to Parveen. She understood the reason she was being chased away. Rahim's family had decided that they did not want her.

It was the most shameful day of her life. She realized that no one could ever shame her in this manner. She stared back at them all: the thin female constable, Nadesan teacher who hid behind the curtain in his home, all those pairs of eyes secretly looking at her from behind their partially open windows. She could fathom a sense of greed in the eyes of the constable.

She looked at the windows of her own home – Rahim's home – and looked at those familiar eyes. She shouted coarse insults. She shouted them so that even the walls in the neighbouring streets heard her. She flung these about freely, wildly, and got into the taxi holding her mother's hand.

Her mother couldn't say a single word until they reached home. Nor could she cry. They spent the rest of the miserable journey in silence.

Talks were held at the jamaat, a separation agreed. When she asked her mother-in-law to return her jewellery, she brazenly lied, claiming that Parveen had already taken them away with her. Rahim repeated the same thing. Jennifer, who was president of the committee of self-help groups, took Parveen to the social welfare department and asked her to record her complaint. After a long investigation, and many, many difficulties, she got her gold jewellery back.

Even thinking about those days pained Parveen... being dragged from pillar to post, being humiliated and shamed. Her husband and his family ensured that she had to undergo all these travails merely in order to belittle her further. Her mother had said, 'Let us not go to the police, we will try to negotiate through the jamaat.'

In the end, thanks to the assurance of the social welfare officials, she successfully filed for a dowry harassment case.

'You may go inside.' Now Parveen returned to the present upon hearing the peon summon her. She and Nafeesa entered the Block Officer's office.

'Come and sit. What can I do for you?' The BO's tone was sympathetic. He was a medium-complexioned, attractive young man, tall and neatly dressed in a manner that could instantly capture anyone's attention. His office was spacious and appeared sparkling new. His table shone with tidily arranged files and beautiful table-top accessories. For some reason, they hesitated to sit in his presence.

Nafeesa started the conversation, still on her feet, 'Sir, in our small village a lot of self-help groups have come together and we have applied for a loan at the bank. We require a little training – can you please make arrangements for that in our village?' It was as if she had memorized these lines, and was now repeating them, or at least that was how it seemed.

The BO silently looked on at them, he must not have been expecting to see two purdah-clad Muslim women coming to ask him for training to be arranged. Once again, he asked them to take a seat, almost as if it was an order. He pressed the bell for the peon to come. 'What's the name of your village?' he asked them. They quickly sat, and Nafeesa repeated the name of the village.

'Yes, I've been there. I've heard they marry girls there really young. The collector often speaks about it.' The women remained silent.

When the peon opened the door, the BO asked him to fetch two cups of tea. Not knowing what to say, the two women kept quiet, surprised that he ordered tea for them. 'In the villages,' he continued, 'they don't seem to realize that child marriage and the marriage of underage girls is a crime. There is no awareness. To prevent it, only people like you can do something. Without someone tipping us off, we cannot come and interfere, you see.' Saying so, he recollected his experiences.

The women did not know how to respond, and listened silently to the BO. For no apparent reason, Parveen remembered that the official's name was Dakshinamoorthy: she had seen the name on a plaque outside his room and assumed that a man with such a name would be old. She remembered someone at the bank had been full of high praise for him. The peon came and placed the tea in front of them. His eyes showed surprise. Parveen felt as if she was somewhat understanding this official's strategy. She saw the tea for what it was: a tactical gesture aiming to turn Parveen and Nafeesa into approvers and collaborators. Irrespective of whether this was a good or bad thing, she liked him. And she liked that he was observing her unveiled face.

Dakshinamoorthy took their silence for assent. He politely asked them to drink their tea, and Parveen observed with the corner of her eye that he was looking at them as they took tentative sips. After so long, she could feel there was a tension and awakening in her body. She enjoyed it very much. She wondered if she had ever felt such a feeling within herself. She was suddenly shy and did not want to catch his glance.

'You go and visit your BDO, say that I recommend you, he will make arrangements for the training. This is my phone number. If any child marriage takes place, give me a ring,' he said, handing out a visiting card each to both of them. 'Of course, your names will not be revealed.'

As they left his room and stepped outside the building, they saw the lady collector get down from her car and walk briskly past them. Her car with the special red light on the top, her cotton sari and haughty walk suddenly pushed Parveen into grief.

She thought, *Will we not get such a life?* She bent her head and took one look at her own black purdah. She was sweating in the relentless afternoon sun, and as she compared the collector's cotton sari and her burqa, for the first time in her life she regretted being born in a village. She cursed her village.

Nafeesa said, 'Hey, Parveen, look at all the marriages in our village. They take place when the girl is fifteen, sixteen years old. How many of these marriages can we report and stop? If anyone finds out about our role in all this, they will kill us.' Then she smiled and said, 'Look at the life that has come to us, we are being offered tea at the BDO's office.

'There's respect indeed for self-help groups. That, too, if Muslim women are involved in a self-help group – no wonder the government is surprised.' Nafeesa was proud of herself.

Parveen was yet to overcome the steady glance of

the young officer. His smart clothes and his personality had captivated her. For the first time in her life, she had met a man who had stirred such restless feelings in her. She felt happy and fulfilled that there was an image of a man she could love in her thoughts. As that day had ended on a fruitful note, she thanked Nafeesa and Allah. But she was troubled, too, by the image of the collector.

As they got into an auto, on their way towards the bus depot, Parveen felt that the heat of the afternoon had grown pleasant.

CHAPTER 37

Sajida longed to be near her mother. Her tongue was dry, every part of her body ached, she felt that she would be much better if only she could rest her head on her mother's lap and go to sleep.

Just as coconut oil freezes into a far end of the bottle in winter, so Sajida too retracted into a corner of the house. Subaida's care and her father's love were not enough. No one could care or love her the way her mother did. She was peeved. In that room where she and her mother and her father and brother had once slept – now there was no one else but her. Everyone was floating in a different direction, scattered. All her anger was directed at her father. She could simply not accept his second marriage which he had entered into for purely selfish reasons. For some reason, now, she drew pleasure from her mother's anger and her revenge, although she felt that Amma really should have taken the children into consideration. Then she started thinking about her mother's ears which would now be free from hearing Asiya's constant complaints. Her mother's ears would find some respite, there was no denying that.

Not having eaten since morning made her stomach uneasy, and she grew nauseous. Three times Subaida Nanni had come inside and asked her to eat, the gruel and lentil chutney was going dry. She wanted to call her mother, but she wasn't sure how to talk to her. She couldn't call from her father's phone. By now, Asiya would have informed her mother, and she would be in tears. If she had a little physical strength she could go to Asiya Nanni's house and make the call from there – but that was not possible now. She lay down for a bit and tried to remember her mother's gentle touch.

All the women of the neighbourhood came and visited her.

Though you have a mother, you are suffering like an orphan, they said. Even in expressing their sympathy, they displayed their anger towards her mother.

That alone was enough to instigate Subaida's fury. She started scolding the visitors recklessly.

Disease was giving way to all types of thoughts. Whenever Saji went to pick out clothes at a shop or to eat at a restaurant, she encountered other children accompanied by both parents. It made her yearn for her own. One day, she saw a girl of her age try on clothes to display to both her parents. The father liked it, the mother did not – she picked out another tunic and asked the daughter to go and try it on. But the father did not approve this time, his face showed dissatisfaction.

Until they both settled on a dress they liked, this scene kept repeating itself, and Sajida kept looking. Sajida did not want to keep living. She had thought a few times about dying.

She wanted to run away from this village to somewhere far away, without any plan of returning. She did not want anybody's looks of sympathy thrown in her direction. This was a firm resolve. She did not look forward to anything except her studies. *If I manage to do that right, it is enough,* she thought. Next year she was going to be in twelfth standard, and take the public exams. She was determined to become a doctor.

She wondered what her mother would be doing at this moment. Only her Aunt Parveen's presence seemed to somewhat compensate for her mother's absence. She wanted to ask her to come in the evening. Even though her father visited her daily, he never spoke to Saji's grandmother – and though she did not know the reason for it, his behaviour upset her. He came only to see his daughter and then went away as if he was a stranger to this house. After he went, there would invariably be a long litany of complaints reeled off by her grandmother.

'What wrong did I do to deserve all this hate from him. Why does the family never have any peace? Shouldn't a mother be worried when bad things keep happening?' she bemoaned to herself.

Saji heard someone at the door. She opened her eyes to see who it could be. It was Jessima! 'Saji, are you fine?' she asked eagerly and then added, 'Your Grandma Asiya wants to see you. She is asking you to come home.'

Subaida who was in the kitchen must have overheard. 'Why does that bald cunt call you home? Stupid bitch, she has separated the mother and the children. What more havoc does she plan to wreak?' She was shouting in anger. 'You must not go there. Your father will not approve.' Sajida and Jessi remained silent. They didn't know what to say.

It was not as if Sajida wanted to go there anyway. It would have helped her call her mother, that was all. She herself knew that the complaints and laments in that house had not come to a stop. Staying in the midst of these women who were crying and shouting and cursing all the time, she realized how brave her mother and Aunt Parveen were. Instead of complaining like this, her grandmothers could do something constructive, she thought – and then chided herself for thinking like a grown-up. She was overthinking.

'Hey, what are you thinking? And why have you not eaten food?' Jessi's voice jolted her back. 'I'm not hungry,' she replied. It had been only two months since she had last seen Jessi, but she had already put on weight, even her skin appeared fair and healthy. Saji could not believe the change, so she stared intently at her friend, before looking back at herself.

She had lost her complexion. She had become thin, just skin and bones…

'I only came back from the madrassa yesterday,' Jessi said. 'On two days' leave. Hey, why have you become like this, so skinny?'

'The food in the hostel is not so good, that's why,' she replied.

Jessi said, 'You could have joined the madrassa along with me. The food is delicious. What are you going to do with all that education? In our village, they will marry us off in two years anyway.'

Sajida did not wish to reply. But she understood something. It would not be easy to get her married. She did not believe that anyone would accept her so easily as a wife or daughter-in-law after hearing the story of her parents. That was one of the only things that seemed to bring her immense joy. It was this line of reasoning that made her feel the continuation of her education was practically guaranteed.

CHAPTER 38

The afternoon sun was blazing. Was she really in Kerala? A persistent doubt – *am I the biggest sinner in this world?* – now appeared to have achieved confirmation.

Mehar felt a thunder descend upon her on hearing that her daughter had typhoid fever. Her mind was filled with a thousand questions. *Has she eaten? Is she taking her medicines properly? How must she be suffering?* She worried, not knowing how to contact her daughter on the phone. And her mother had said that even she had been unable to meet Sajida. And how could her mother enter Subaida's house to look at her granddaughter, after all?

Parveen called her this morning. 'Don't worry, she's getting better. I will look after her.' She had hesitantly added, 'If it is possible please come.'

Mehar called Habi and told him, 'My daughter is unwell. I must go back to the village.' She was afraid of approaching him so directly as he often lost his temper these days –if she spoke about her children, or if she wept, he would get angry and say, 'I do not like coming home to this hell.'

Before, he used to say, 'Bring the children here, keep them with you. Who is saying anything against that?' And she would reply, 'How will they allow a girl who has come of age to stay in the house of a man who is not a relative?'

From morning she had neither cooked not eaten. She wondered what sort of mother she must be if she could not even take care of her children. She wondered if she must stay alive. These thoughts ran through her head like a sharp knife. From the moment she had thought about her own starving children, she could not bear the idea of cooking for a stranger here. She had stopped cooking in order to navigate her guilty consciousness. Somehow, she must go to the village today, she decided. She was impatient for Habi to come back home.

That night he came home much later than usual. These days, he was hardly motivated to come home at all, afraid of encountering her weeping, so he had made a plan to spend as much time as possible outside the house. He also felt the discomfort and anxiety of visiting someone else's home when he did return to his own place.

Although Mehar's tears and sighs were forcing him to confront a mental conflict, he was unable to prevent his own anger. He was afraid that his outburst would have an adverse reaction on things. So it seemed right to avoid going home.

Tonight, he entered in a state of apprehension. He peeped into the bedroom, wondering where Mehar was. She was sitting in a corner, her head buried in her hands. It made him feel sick.

'What are you doing?' he asked her gently in a supportive voice.

She raised her head, looked at him and said, 'I need to go to the village, it seems Saji has typhoid.'

For Mehar, who lay weeping in bed every night, today had offered up a fresh reason. To console her, he said, 'There are others there to look after her, is it essential that you go?' He said that in spite of his better judgement. 'No, I must go,' she insisted madly. She seemed not to even be listening to what he was saying. 'No, I must go.' As if she was clinging to these very words.

'Onam is coming, I need to look after the shop. Can you go back alone? I cannot come with you,' he said. He was suppressing his anger, speaking through clenched teeth. 'First, please serve the food, I'm hungry,' he said.

She replied, 'I did not cook.'

Driven by hunger and pent-up anger, he flew into a rage. 'What the fuck are you doing all day then?' he shouted vehemently and left the house. Mehar sat for a long time in stunned silence.

CHAPTER 39

Sajida woke to the sound of the alarm. For a moment, she was confused as to where she was, in the darkness. She felt the bed beside her for her mother and was fooled. Realizing that she was back in the hostel, she sat up and sighed.

It was bitter to think that her mother was at her own mother's place. Then, the thought of her father being with his second wife made her feel even worse. She wanted to die.

She chastised herself. *Why these morbid thoughts so early in the morning? After all, I have come here to study.* She got out of bed and walked towards the bathroom. She started splashing water on her face, deciding to finish her fajr prayers and leave her burdens to Allah. In the early light of morning, as she proceeded to perform her prayers, she remembered crying to her mother on the first night in the hostel.

Do you want me or is your husband more important to

you?

She realized her own helplessness and continued her prayers.

CHAPTER 40

Mehar sighed in relief when she realized that what she believed had been an endless journey was now, finally, coming to an end. It did not make her happy or sad, it only made her tired as she counted the steps she had taken. The journey did not appear to be something that could be easily transcended and she worried about staying stuck, even at this point.

She had left without telling anyone at home. She did not take anything with her except a purse, and yet she felt a heavy burden upon her shoulders. The thought that the path she had carved for herself was a one-way journey made her feel peaceful now.

In the life that she had lived for a year, the thought of having lost proximity to her children had made her extremely sad. She had wept and wondered if shedding tears would undo the damage. This question seemed to mock her. Now, she was escaping the life of a corpse. She felt her heart overflow with thoughts of Sajida.

CHAPTER 41

Hasan entered the house, asking 'Where is Parveen?', and Nanni replied smartly, 'Salaam alaykum!'

Hasan returned the salutation belatedly. He asked her how she was and sat down near her on the day-bed and grasped her hand. She touched his face and felt his beard. 'Why do you have such a long beard,' she said, 'why can't you trim it?'

'Don't ask me to remove my beard Nanni, you will become a sinner to Allah. On Judgement Day he will send you to hell,' Hasan replied.

Nanni kept quiet. It was better to remain silent than to talk to him. Parveen greeted her brother. His voice grew hoarse as he challenged her: 'I hear you have joined some group and taken out a bank loan? You keep going to the bank and BDO office and collector's office?'

She was quiet. He knew everything anyway so what was the point in answering. Her silence made him even angrier. 'I keep instructing the entire village: women must remain at home, it is haram for them to get a loan at the bank or give interest. Even you have read all this in the Quran, where has your intelligence gone? I'm your brother, I am trying to reform society, I'm trying to make sure that people keep to the right path, and you are doing the exact opposite. What to say!'

Parveen looked at him intently, but she had lost interest in his words. He had shrunk, he appeared broken; his beard was long. When he was young, there was no boy in the village who could keep up with his zeal for watching movies and listening to songs. When a new film song was released, he would be the first to possess a cassette tape. His enthusiasm, his dancing, none of this could even be captured in words. After returning from Saudi Arabia, and on completing his Hajj, his personality and behaviour had completely changed. He had become like an old man who did not have any attachment to life.

'Why can't I hear a reply?' he scolded her now.

'Nothing,' she said, 'staying home is not easy, it does things to my mind. That is all. I did not go alone, some other women came with me, so what is wrong with that?'

How would he realize what it would mean for

a woman like her to stay inside the house for years, how much she must hate it, how it would corrode her mental state. She did not know if he could even comprehend her situation, and yet she replied with the honest truth, fully aware that to him they would only be empty words.

'So if your mind is not fine, pray, read the Quran, ask Allah to give you peace of mind. But you don't have faith in all that. When people come and tell me that my sister is roaming around, behaving like a loose woman, I lose my respect and dignity. Forget everything you have done so far, go to the jamaat three times a week, take part in the woman's jamaat, volunteer for that, then your mind will be clean.

'On the Day of Judgement, Allah will ask me, "Did you show the right path to your sister?" That is why I came. To fulfil my duty. Salaam. I'm going now.' He left as abruptly as he had come.

He must have been very angry because she had not offered even one word of regret or apology. On the one hand, she was relieved that he was gone. On the other hand, she was perturbed by the knowledge that because he only believed in a few things, he was torturing himself and others. There was so much rigidity in his outlook, but there was so much that was simply not in his control...

She wondered how it was possible for him to change his very nature and claim that he was living for the afterlife? He had once been so full of happiness and vigour, now he had bundled everything away. What sort of life was that? If confronted, he said that 'music was haram, cinema was haram.' She felt that so much of his self-control was an exercise in cruelty.

For the past few years, this was how a few men in the village had behaved, acting in an extreme manner, wanting to transform the village and protect its women. She did not know how to interpret all this. She did not recollect it being quite so bad earlier, wasn't this a recent occurrence? What was it a reaction to? Before, women would just use some loose white cloth to hide their bodies; today, even little children were wearing black veils that covered their very faces. Girls were being sent only to the madrassa, held back from pursuing a decent education. Parveen grew irritated when she thought that literally every house had one young man who had taken it upon himself to banish the evils of shirk. This was the problem in every house. She knew, because the women would complain to each other about such men.

Although she felt love and sympathy towards her brother, she was again relieved that she was not living under his roof anymore. Just on this one day, his preaching had been sufficient to push her into deep mental turbulence. She went towards the kitchen, trying to move forward with the day, even as she sighed deeply.

She pitied his ignorance, his thoughtless manner of leaving the minute the purpose of his visit was completed – instead of asking about her, about the family's problems, about Sajida's health or even trying to resolve his own rift with their mother. These details of domestic life simply did not seem to relate to him.

With his dreams about the afterlife and heaven, he seemed not to pay attention to any of the goings-on in this life. She remembered that there had been a call from the BDO's office earlier in the day about training to be given for preparing sottu neelam. 'The officer has asked us to offer a lot of training workshops in your village, madam. He said that you came and made a request,' the person on the phone had said.

She was excited, 'Is that so? Did he mention the name of our group?'

'He even mentioned your name, madam, so we are coming tomorrow.'

She knew the BO's number by heart. Even though she never spoke to him, every day she would pick up the phone and attempt to dial his number. Then shyness would take over, and she would regret not having a good reason to call. Today, though she felt there was a perfectly valid excuse, she still felt painfully shy. She did not want him to suspect that she was calling because she was attracted to him, she wanted him to feel that she had a legitimate reason to want to talk to him.

Well, so, what if he knows that I like him. That way, he could reveal what he feels about me. She was caught up in a web of her confused emotions. She decided to call him after the training programme was completed the next day. This made her feel light.

CHAPTER 42

Mehar was determined to remain here irrespective of what happened now. There was no hell apart from being separated from her own children − the remarriage and the following year had provided her with the insight that there was nothing worse. Asiya's complaints and laments and curses would do nothing to her now, she was ready to face anything that came to pass. Asiya asked, 'How did you come? Why did you come? Did you come alone, on your own?' Mehar knew that no answers would put an end to her mother's questions, so she kept silent.

Mehar was making the choice to become a permanent resident in that room filled with long sighs. No one could oust her from its cool darkness now. She believed that she would once again enjoy the intimacy and happiness she had once shared with her children. She began to wait for it, patiently yearning. She firmly believed that time would see her win.

She also wanted her mother to understand that nothing would shake her faith in this. Even the thought that her children would return for the holidays shortly made her float in ecstasy – there was simply no other thought. She had travelled for an entire day on her own, not knowing the direction of her journey, the route, the language… All she had was the address written down in English on the back of an envelope posted by a ready-made clothing businessman from the village. She had gone to various shopkeepers and asked them for directions. She thought of her last-minute decision to bring along that envelope with her, how it had been a godsend. She changed buses three times. A few people saw the address and then gave her directions in Tamil. She realized that wearing the burqa was a protective measure, a talisman that kept her safe since no one could see even her face, even though she suffered from the miserable heat. She once again thought of Saji's pain, and it had helped her forget the discomfort of her own journey.

During Saji's typhoid fever, she had stayed silent because she felt that she could not travel alone. And Habi had told her that he could not leave the shop during the festive season.

For a week she was in tears, she starved, she was a mad woman yielding to her plight. Habi came home, took one look at the state she was in, and either because he was afraid or simply didn't like what he saw, he had stopped coming home. He spent his nights in the shop instead, and she could sense that even he regretted this entanglement. Seeing her float about the rooms of the house night and day had terrified him. Sometimes, he was beset by the fear that she would do something drastic in his absence – and so he didn't go to the shop, he just stayed home to prevent anything untoward. Her body shook when she thought of that city and the isolation in which she lived. It was hell. It did not matter where she ran or what she did, or where she retreated, everything seemed to resemble a shadow of hell. She was angry with Allah. She wondered if He was subjecting only her to such grief.

She remembered how much she had suffered from her mother's laments and the village ostracizing her. But this new place that she had gone to, and which she had now fled, it had become an even greater hell.

At least here, in the village, her children were with her, there was no possibility of that in Kerala. She had now come to the firm decision that she did not need anything beyond her own children.

She felt her heart flutter. They were going to return home in a few days. They would be with her. Happiness overflowed upon realizing that she no longer had to ask a stranger's permission to call her own children, or beg to be allowed to visit them.

She was relieved that her mother was not screaming as she had anticipated. Perhaps Asiya, too, understood the mental difficulties Mehar and her children had endured. Her mother must know now what Saji had gone through during her long illness, she thought.

She heard a knock on the door and her mother's voice asking, 'Who is there?' Mehar was afraid. She knew that the women of the village would have got wind of her return — they would visit just to report it to the others and gossip among themselves later. She decided not to see anyone who visited.

'Come, Parveen.' She heard her mother's voice and the door bolt being unlocked. She sat up on the bed. She gathered her loose hair and tried to tie it up. The hair was tangled and the effort hurt – so much of it had fallen out, only a handful remained.

'Hey, why have you become so thin?' She heard Parveen's voice as she looked up. All the tears that she had suppressed so far gushed forth like a burst dam. She embraced Parveen as she wept.

In those tears, in that embrace, she could sense a peace that had been absent until then. The incomparable peace that comes when one slowly counts and retrieves all that was lost. A peace that could not be described.

CHAPTER 43

Hasan felt irrepressibly happy on hearing the news of Mehar's return. This was nothing surprising, he thought, who could ever live with her? She was a demoness, she was a cry-baby,; where else could she find a place as comfortable as the one he had provided her? Someday, she would have to answer to God for the betrayal she had caused him – she must have come to the same realization herself. He was very satisfied indeed.

Just because a man does something, how could she think that a woman too could do the same? What sort of a haughty cunt she must be to have done so? And because a bad word had entered his mind, he asked for forgiveness from Allah. *She left the children and went away, so why the fuck was she back now.* For some reason, anger suddenly weighed him down, and thinking about all this did not make things easier.

He was not unaware that he had lost credibility in

the village the moment he had married a second time. But she was responsible for his second marriage, was she not? If he advised her to wear her burqa properly, she would not talk to him for an entire week. She would keep a long face if he asked her not to wear lipstick because it was not meant for family women. She would sulk, 'All the women in this village wear it anyway.'

She totally lacked brains. Was he like other men in the village? He couldn't touch her at night for fear that a child could be conceived. What sort of a life was it? To use condoms with her? Why was she his wife then?

He consoled himself by blaming her for everything. What was the point of all this now. She had come back at the end of it all. *Let her now sit in a corner. She caused me endless shame, we should not let her go without revenge, she must weep until her dying day,* he thought to himself.

Then he thought how despite this, even he was bereft of happiness. All his respect and stature within the village was gone – he lived life as a walking corpse. Then, he wondered if the many extra hours he had spent at the mosque and in the tasks of the tablighi jamaat were a result of his own increased religiosity, or an attempt to reclaim his lost pride and social standing within the village. He tried his best to refute the second reason, because it filled him with shame.

He prayed to Allah and asked for forgiveness. Now, even his mother and sister had no fear of him; they, too, were rebelling and doing whatever pleased them. Everything was lost. All that he had now was his children and Khadija. He did not want to lose his grip over them, at the very least. Khadija, a poor and simple girl, obeyed his every word.

It was his children who needed to be safeguarded from Mehar's shadow even, he thought. He wanted her to cry and cry in repentance for the mistakes she had committed. He felt his blood boil, his head spin. He leaned his head on the chair and put his feet up, sitting in a more relaxed posture.

CHAPTER 44

More than three hundred self-help groups from the village came together to deliver the training programme. Those who came from the BDO's office gave workshops on how to make clothes whiteners, candles and paper bags. Because it was a Sunday, they chose a large classroom at the government school for these classes. Parveen and Nafeesa took care of all the organizational tasks. Both felt great pride that they had made a request to the BDO, and helped bring all this about. They called up the head of every self-help group and asked them to attend along with their members. It was very hot indoors, and Parveen had a horrible headache. The workshop was meant to finish by one in the afternoon. If she could eat lunch and lie down for a while her headache would subside. Nafeesa was coming towards her, her large frame like a billowing cloth moving in the wind.

She was beaming. 'Nice turnout,' she said. 'It's

the heat that's killing us. It doesn't matter how much water we drink, I'm always thirsty.' She breathed in deeply, sighed.

'Yes, that must be why even I have a headache. Now if we take the initiative to organize one or two meetings in the village, there will be some money in the hands of our women, and they will have an opportunity to step outside the home.' Parveen's eyes shone with hope. It was contagious; Nafeesa, too, caught it on. She felt that something she, too, had always complained about, had finally materialized thanks to Parveen.

Ten years ago, Nafeesa had lost her husband to tuberculosis and she did not know where her next meal would come from. But this job, and the many people she had met along the way, made her happy. Using government loans, a group of women belonging to her self-help group were rearing cattle and goats. They were given money on loan to start some small business, and so they could get by. What more was necessary, she thought.

Parveen saw the smile on Nafeesa's face. 'What are you daydreaming about?' she asked as she heard a car in the distance, then saw a white Ambassador car approaching towards the school. She looked at Nafeesa in surprise. They were certain that it was the

BO's car. Although they were too surprised to know quite what to do, they ran towards the school gates. Parveen pulled the purdah over her head. Her whole body trembled ecstatically, and she felt her heart beat a hundred times faster.

The car stopped upon seeing the women. The BO got out slowly and returned their greeting. 'How is the training coming along?' he asked Parveen. She seemed to have lost her capacity to speak, she hung her head in shyness. Nafeesa stepped in, 'Everything is going good sir, thank you so much. Now you have also come—' She, too, seemed to be tongue-tied.

'I'm happy,' he said – and then looking at Parveen, he asked Nafeesa, 'Why is your associate not speaking at all?'

'No sir – thanks – we can go inside, please come' – she struggled to get the words out. Parveen walked ahead, as Nafeesa walked by his side and answered all his questions.

They walked under the shade of a row of neem trees in order to reach the classroom. Parveen could hear her own heartbeat as clearly as if it was one of a sound in the quiet of night. She could feel the invasive glance of the pair of eyes on her back. Perhaps because of her anxiety or her shyness, she felt that she was walking with a certain impatience. From the simple fact that he was responding to Nafeesa's long sentences with single-word answers, Parveen could easily surmise that all his attention was on herself.

His visit made the entire gathering happy. The staff of the BDO's office who were present there welcomed their superior official with excitement, and they tried to compete with one another for his attention, reciting pertinent details of the workshops. Parveen observed the drama that was offset by power. Just the thought that such a powerful man liked her made her feel hot, feel proud.

Nafeesa did not fail to observe their intimacy exchanged solely through glances and oppressive silences which seemed to hold a host of conversations. It was not difficult for her to read this.

That night, in the aloneness of her room, Parveen satisfied the craving of many days. It did not matter whether her eyes were open or closed – his imposing form, his eyes, his speech – these were forever present and driving her to desperation. She took to looking at herself in the mirror. In a hopeless face, she could see – for the first time – countless hopes and the brightness that came with them.

CHAPTER 45

As Sajida stepped out of the car and into Subaida Nanni's home, she once again heard Hasan's voice from the car. 'Do you remember everything I said? I will come later.' He drove off.

Sajida hated him.

She wondered why schools had vacations. She wondered if she even had a place to call home to return to, now that the hostel was closed for summer holidays. For at least the next forty days she had to stay in the village, though even the thought of it filled her with bitterness. *They are going to throw us around like a football. They do whatever they please, but only we lose our peace.* She was pissed off.

All the things her father had said during the journey home made her feel that her head would explode. Things about how her mother had betrayed him, how she was unloving – everything was aimed to inculcate and foster a hatred towards her.

Her room-mates had been looking forward to going home, but there was nothing here that made her happy. Where else to go? She was afraid that she would go mad. She feared her parents' petty point-scoring would somehow put an end to her studies.

This year had been okay. Only if she got really good marks next year, would she be eligible for a medical student's seat under the quota. If the family problems came to an end, at least by then, things would be great. As usual, she left it to Allah to solve her problems – though nowadays, even her belief in Allah was shaky. Since the day she had been old enough, she had never missed a single prayer. It was the same with her mother, and both her grandmothers.

In Jessi's house, her mother never even prayed. But all the trouble seemed to arrive only at Sajida's family's door. Everyone else was fine, Allah seemed to test only them. The more she thought about it, the more depressed she felt. Even as she entered the house, her mind was consumed by various thoughts. She recalled that Hasan had explicitly banned her from seeing her mother or speaking with her.

Even when you had typhoid, she could not come and visit you. Is she a mother – who does not visit her child even when they are at death's door? Sajida was disgusted by his implication. Her father's voice had been overflowing with the hatred he tried to instigate, and his silence confirmed to her that he was upset she had not responded to his hateful rant.

She walked to her room, extremely stressed and sad, dropping her school bag on the floor. Clothes were scattered all over the room. The bedspread and floor were covered with a thin layer of dust. Ashraf must have come and gone for his holidays – he always threw his clothes around in such a manner. 'Idiot,' she scolded him gently under her breath.

Just the thought of her brother brought fresh grief. It had been at least two months since she had last seen him. When he was on leave, she could not come; when she came on leave, he could not come – that was always how things went. That's why, she suddenly remembered, she had been eagerly awaiting the summer holiday.

Sajida removed her burqa and put it in the washing basket, then went to the kitchen to see if she could find something to eat. Her grandmother was not in the habit of cooking for herself. She also suffered from arthritis, so could hardly do much around the house. She never cooked anything that she or her brother liked. She would say, *Call up your father and ask him to buy it from the hotel-shop.*

Ashraf would tease her: *What do you mean*

hotel-shop? Just say 'hotel'.

She would respond: *I'm not educated like you.*

There was nothing to eat at home, Saji was hungry. Her grandmother Subaida was asleep, completely unaware that she was here.

Amma had returned to Asiya's home. She wanted to go and meet her, but then she remembered her father's threat. She would go the next day. He would lose his cool completely if he learnt that she had visited her mother so soon. She was tired now, dizzy with hunger. She tried to sleep on the dust-laden bed. In sleep, there appeared a dream where she heard her mother weeping and Asiya Nanni grumbling, *You must marry* – she was pressuring her mother, who stood in a forest, crying and crying, she was trying to explain something...

Unable to bear the heaviness of the dreams that chased her, Saji woke with a start – and was frightened by the darkness in the room.

CHAPTER 46

Parveen finally dialled the number she had memorized by heart. She had decided to do it in the middle of a thousand deliberations and hesitations. Her heart beat faster than ever. On hearing his hello, which pushed her into a nervous frenzy, she replied quickly, 'Vanakkam sir, this is Parveen.' Her words betrayed her excitement.

'Yes, tell me.' His voice showed enthusiasm – she had anticipated this, but it still made her happy. 'Nothing sir, I just wanted to thank you.'

'Oh, no, there's no need for that, we did our job. It is you who needs to be praised by us, it is not easy to gather so many women for this sort of thing in your village.' She felt that this was a genuine appreciation of her efforts to create opportunities for the women of her village.

'Do continue to carry out the excellent work you are doing. Slowly, we must also create awareness against child marriage through the women's group, and if ever the need arises, do tip us off.' And then he said, 'Is there something further you'd like to discuss? If you have some errand in the area, do drop by at my office.' His eagerness, his brash boldness, seemed to do things to her. She did not know what to say. 'Hmm, hmm,' Parveen murmured in an effort to sound relaxed, but then she felt even that came out in a cloying manner. She quickly added, 'Of course sir, we will speak later,' and then she hung up.

She could feel that his speech was very official. She tried to explain this away – perhaps because he was in the office. However things stood, speaking to him had made her irrepressibly happy.

She simultaneously encountered two very different thoughts: did one need this petty gratification? And: what was so wrong in wanting it? She justified the call, telling herself that the vivacious happiness it gave her was enough.

It was not permanent. It was not love. It was not going to go anywhere, it was not going to evolve into anything. But she was unabashed in admitting that both her body and mind needed this excitement. For the dreams that came to her that night, she wished to provide some kind of faith.

CHAPTER 47

On knowing that Sajida had come, Mehar's heart danced with joy. She was waiting for her to visit. Saji knew her mother would burst into tears if she saw how thin she had become. She timidly stepped into her house which was only the next street along from Subaida's. On her way, she had decided that she would delay removing her burqa for as long as possible.

When she saw her mother sitting on the water tank in the corner of the house, it was Sajida who was shocked and saddened. Mehar had dried up and wilted. The face of the mother she had known until then, and the face she was seeing now – there were great changes and chasms of time between those faces. On seeing her, Mehar embraced her tightly and wept.

'I have come away my darling. I've come just as you asked. You see, I will never go anywhere, I will never leave you behind.' She was saying all this loudly even as she wept.

Mother and daughter took turns to touch each other. Each wept on seeing the other's state. Asiya was watching over everything with a heavy silence. It took a great deal of effort on her part to not express her own sorrow, but she was careful not to intrude on the sweetness of their interaction. She observed that Mehar's tears seemed to signal that she was finally free of all the stress she had been under.

Mehar was relieved that Hasan had not succeeded in turning her daughter against her, despite all the damning things he must have said during her absence. She had felt that the day her children began hating her would be the day she would have to stop living. Today, she was able to break free from that thought.

Even as she was relieved to see Sajida, the thought of Ashraf troubled Mehar. She was unable to talk about the matter openly, yet both Sajida and Asiya sensed her worry. Only Sajida knew the extent to which her father had said vile and outrageous things about their mother to stir hatred in the hearts of her two children. She wondered what her own state of mind might have been if her mother had not returned – whether she would have been filled with anger and disgust for her. It was possible. She was determined, somehow, to make her little brother come and meet their mother.

—

Later that day, Ashraf was riding a cycle through the
street. It was a cycle hired from Amir's shop, the cost
of hire five rupees for an hour, which his father duly
paid. While he was speeding through the streets,
on seeing Asiya Nanni's house he slowed down and
turned away. If his mother was there, she would call
him; if he did not go, she would cry; if he spoke to
her, father would get upset, he would scold him. He
would not give him the money to ride the cycle.
Why, then, get into trouble?

He wanted to speed along in the cycle until his
one hour was up. He wanted, even, to ride his father's
moped. When he had asked his father, he would say:
You are too small, your legs will not reach the pedal.

He thought that he had grown taller now and, if he
implored enough, perhaps his father would let him.
So, he would not do anything that could upset his
father. He loved his mother. He did not like that fat
lady Khadija. Whenever he looked, there she was, in
the front of the car, next to his father. He would feel
like throwing a stone at her. Before, only he would sit
at the front seat, not even letting his mother or Saji
sit there. And now, his father was letting that fatty sit
there, and it made him very, very angry.

As planned, he had cycled towards Subaida Nanni's

house, because Saji had said that she wanted something from the shop. He stood on the street and called
out to her, 'Saji, Saji'. Subaida stepped outside and
said, 'You must call your sister Akka, and not by her
name.'

'Ha, ha. She's Akka, I see. Some big sister!' He
once again called her by name. Mischief shone across
his face – it was clear that he wanted to annoy his
grandmother. She felt like chuckling to herself,
secretly proud of his defiance. She went inside the
house calling Saji and asked her to go and meet her
brother who was yelling outside.

She was complaining to herself under her breath.
'This Hasan is still not talking to me. It has been more
than six months. Has Allah said that he must not talk
to me? He talks of ibaddat all the time – but does he
know of any religious teaching that tells someone to
stop talking to their mother?'

There was a lot of work to be done, but her body
simply refused to cooperate. The servant had come,
swept the floor, washed the dishes, then went away.
Now, Subaida had to cook. She had to put the clothes
in the washing machine. She had to feed the children
properly. They were merely skin and bones because
of the bad food and lack of care at the hostel. Once,
they had been two lucky children; and now they had

neither mother nor father.

A man can be as horrible as he pleases, but what makes a woman behave like that? She could have lived like a queen with both her children. So much spite and so much arrogance that she got married and went away! Was she eating rice or shit? Stupid bitch, may evil befall her. Allah knows all, did He give her peace? She must have suffered cruelty with her new husband, why else would she have run away? Allah lives.

She scolded Mehar with all the hatred she could summon.

Yesterday, when her daughter Parveen came home, she had complained to her. 'I'm old, and I'm the one looking after the children. Is it even possible for me? He does not want to let them near their mother – he wants me to keep them. My knees and calves pain all the time. My own son hates me. Do you think these two kids are going to be nice to me?' She was on the brink of tears. Parveen sat there in silence. She did not know how to console her mother. She understood her brother's idiotic behaviour. He would do exactly as he pleased, imposing his beliefs on others.

And in order to do that, he would claim this was the sharia, that this was what the Quran said, that this was law. He was not the type of man who admitted to his mistakes. He would justify it all with religion.

This was his only topic of conversation. Nothing else could seep into his mind. And now, it appeared he had lost all his loved one because of his rigid actions, his harshness and his cruelty.

Last week Hussein Uncle had come to visit Subaida and Hasan had happened to be home. 'Well Uncle, you used to boast about bringing up your children in the most disciplined manner but I heard that your children were in the cinema theatre in town last week. Your daughter Ayesha and your son Yusuf. It seems your daughter was wearing a burqa without even properly covering her face!'

The man had been quite taken aback. His face betrayed his sadness at being at the receiving end of Hasan's preaching. 'Oh, is that so. I don't know. I don't believe it's possible...' He was feeling very embarrassed. Even his mother had said to him several times, 'Why does it bother you how other people in the village lead their lives. Keep your mouth and your ass shut. And keep your religiosity to yourself!'

'Allah has asked us to bring on the right path those who stray and those who are on the wrong path. Why are you women interfering in all this? You mind your own business. What do you know about outside matters?'

Parveen thought of his excitement in going to see

a film on its release day. That was before he had gone
to Saudi Arabia. He used to be so happy, so enthusiastic. She felt great pity for him. Why did he torture
himself by giving up what he once loved so much?
She wondered if this was why he was always showing
his hatred and anger towards others, frustrated by his
own illicit wants – which were, in fact, such ordinary
joys. Unable to give any answers to Subaida, she left
her mother's house and slowly started making her way
towards her own.

CHAPTER 48

A meeting of the presidents and secretaries of the various self-help groups was being held. Parveen, Nafeesa, her neighbour Abida, Bukanisha, Rafeeqa and Basheera had come together.

Basheera asked, 'Are just the few of us enough?'

'The others didn't come – what can we do about it?' Nafeesa replied.

A WhatsApp message flashed on Abida's phone. 'Look at this, my husband is asking if I would like this fish.' She showed it to the others.

Nafeesa said, licking her lips, 'Sakkara meen – it will be tasty.' So Abida texted back, 'Okay.'

Nafeesa smiled, 'Times have changed so much. Now we are able to select fish just by looking at a photo from the shop.'

Basheera replied, 'Do you think only fish is chosen in this manner? Even from the garments shop, photos are sent and selections are made. This is what my husband does.' She laughed.

'Everything has changed since these phones. In the old days, if we gossiped about somebody on the phone, they would only go and tell the concerned person the next day. Nowadays, they use the recording feature on their phone the minute you call them. And then they play it back to the person who is being gossiped about! Last week a fight got totally out of hand between my brother's wife Shyna and her brother's wife Mumtaj. Someone bitched around,' Abida relished narrating this piece of information, and laughed.

This was true, Parveen thought to herself, everything had changed since the women had got their hands on mobile phones. After all, she was using it to talk to the handsome officer!

Rafeeqa said, 'Let me show you something—' She fumbled through her video gallery and pressed play. The women gathered around her to take a closer look. It was a video of a sex scene!

'Do we really need this shit?' Nafeesa pulled a face.

'Oh no – but this is also the kind of thing that circulates on WhatsApp. If anyone wants this video, tell me, I will forward it,' she said.

Abida quickly asked for it. 'Yes, send it, let's see what it's about,' her voice affecting a certain disinterest. She had adopted that tone so no one would feel she was eager to see the video. Parveen, too, wanted to ask, but she felt shy and embarrassed. The women would wonder why she was asking to see the video when she did not have a husband. Almost as if she had read Parveen's innermost thoughts, Rafeeqa announced, 'I've sent the video to all of you,' and laughed.

Parveen felt nervous. She heard the phone beep once the message reached her but she sat in her chair as if she was completely unbothered. She was very aware that Basheera and Abida were experts in reading the smallest facial gesture, so she should not give off the impression that she was eager to see what the video was about. She could imagine what they would report back to the others. *She's dry and withered without a husband. That's why she was so excited about the video! She was so happy to get it, you can tell she could look at it and... you know...*

These days, more than anything, it was the thought of the officer Moorthy that made her excited. For the first time in her life she was experiencing such a feeling, ecstatic and electrified by the idea that she did not know if this was love or desire or a mix of the two. She seemed incapable of responding to the world around her because she was lost in her own interior world, imagining her secret erotic encounter... The sounds of the women laughing among themselves suddenly reined her in.

Abida asked her, 'What are you daydreaming about, hey – these women are talking all kinds of nonsense.'

'Oh, nothing!' she said, flushed.

She had wanted to make Mehar sign up to one of these self-help groups. She would observe her former sister-in-law spend each day at home with no means of escape, weeping to herself. Parveen felt that if Mehar managed to step out of the house it would help her mental well-being, but Mehar did not agree. 'I don't want anything. I don't want to step out. I'm happy to live and die inside these four walls,' she said.

In their stubbornness, and refusal to budge even slightly from their decisions, both Mehar and Asiya were alike. She had not probed the matter further.

Rafeeqa said, 'Next week is the marriage of Mumtaj's daughter. We can meet the week after.' Then the day's meeting dispersed with more chatter. Normally these meetings took place in Parveen's house. Amina would stay in her room, listening intently to whatever was being said.

Today, she was sitting in the living room and listening to their talk. When the women left, Parveen asked her: 'Why are you listening to all their silly nonsense. You should lie down, get some rest.'

'I should pass my time somehow, shouldn't I? It's not fun to sleep, wake up, sleep, wake up!' Amina Nanni's face was bright and happy. 'Ha, if this was my mother Subaida, she would have endlessly been shouting.' Parveen laughed as she made this remark.

'Leave her, she's a total idiot.' Amina replied and then flashed a big smile. Her smile was contagious. Parveen realized that a change had swept over her – and even Amina could deduce this, though she did not know the reason behind it.

'Have you heard Nanni, Mumtaj's daughter is getting married.' Parveen was conveying the news but, in her mind, she was busy making a calculation. Mumtaj's daughter would be about thirteen years old now. Until half a year ago, she had been riding a cycle on the streets along with the boys. Mumtaj had been waiting for her to come of age so that she could her marry her off to her elder sister's son.

My sister has only one son. Lots of property. I have only one daughter. It's true that the groom is much older, but so what? My elder sister was waiting for my little girl to come of age. Mumtaj had told this to Nanni herself a while ago. Parveen recollected it now.

Mumtaj's elder sister Farida's son was in Saudi Arabia. He was twenty-nine or thirty. Suddenly,

Parveen was irritated.

'What sort of marriage is that? What a damned village!' she cursed loudly. Nanni could understand the meaning behind Parveen's outburst. She silently nodded.

CHAPTER 49

Saji tried to reason with Ashraf, 'Hey, take pity on Amma. She carried us for ten months in her stomach to give birth to us.'

'So. So, did I ask her to do that?' he countered.

'Idiot. You are not visiting mother merely because father asked you not to. Why do you listen to everything he says? Look at me,' Saji said.

She could see he was unhappy, despite his best efforts to look unbothered. 'What can I do? He tells me not to go, you tell me to go. He is beating me and when I go there, all I hear is crying. Get lost.' He busied himself with his kite-making.

'What are you saying? You can look at your kite later!' She gently rapped his head.

'Why are you beating me, you crazy!' he lifted his hand to hit her back. Saji moved away and went and stood on top of the bed. 'I'm sparing you because you are my sister, otherwise...' he warned her. He went back to focusing on his kite.

After her return from the hostel, Sajida's health had improved considerably. But Ashraf was such a pain. He only ever wanted to play, he just would not eat. If he stayed with their mother, she would somehow make him eat. It seemed he was on a mission to while away as much time as possible playing stupid games.

Cycling, the motorbike, flying a kite – he spent all day in the sun, getting darker and scrawnier. When she looked at him even Saji felt like crying – so how could mother restrain her tears? She understood that his intention was to simply stay outdoors as much as possible – avoiding the women of the house and all their clamour.

What could be done? He was unruly and not willing to listen. On top of that, Amma cried endlessly for him. Even if Sajida had wanted a little peace during the holidays, it did not seem likely now. She decided to talk to Parveen Kuppi about it when she visited, as she usually did in the evenings – perhaps Ashraf would listen to her.

Sajida decided that she must find an excuse to make him stay at home when Parveen was around. She looked at his thin arms as he kept fussing about with his kite. She sighed. 'Hey, why do you look at me like that?' he asked. These days he behaved like an old man. Same with his speech. Perhaps listening to all the things that Amma and Aththa said about each other had meant he had lost his innocence. Hadn't Sajida been forced to grow up too, after all?

That night as they were sleeping alone in their room he whispered into the dark, 'What Aththa did was wrong, but why did Amma do the same thing, you tell me, is it not wrong?'

'No da, mother was not willing. She said no. I was the one who listened to Asiya Nanni and told her to do it. I am a fool.'

'No, don't say that… The two of us will study well and take up good jobs.'

'Yes, you must study properly,' Saji whispered, smiling to herself. And then, 'Do you like hostel food?'

'Hell, no! It's disgusting. I don't eat that stuff.'

'I don't like it either. That's why I got typhoid.' And as she said that, her expression one of sadness, he took her hand and placed it on his chest.

'Ashraf, don't worry, I will take care of you,' she said. To hide their longing and their helplessness, the children hugged each other.

'Remember those days when I used to sleep lying between mother and father. I miss that. I want to go out together, all of us, just like before. We were so happy, no?'

'During these holidays, all my friends have gone with their parents somewhere – only we cannot go,' she said.

And Ashraf asked, 'You think we will never live together again?'

His voice was breaking. 'No, never,' she said.

That night Saji did not sleep. She thought how they would clean their own rooms in the morning. She pictured the two of them putting their clothes in order in the cupboard. For the last four days, Ashraf had not taken a shower. He was still walking around in the same pair of clothes. Who could tell him to go and bathe himself? If Amma was here, she would have done so. Only yesterday, she had observed that for the last six months Ashraf had been using the same toothbrush – and she asked for a new brush to be bought from the shop. Subaida was not aware of all these details. For everything, her only answer was: 'I am an old woman.'

Thinking of all this, Saji felt her father was to blame for everything, and she felt an irrepressible anger towards him.

CHAPTER 50

The street was bathed in light. Mehar was sitting at the entrance of her house, watching. Even if it was the hottest part of the day, Ashraf would be on his cycle out on the streets. When he came near, she would run into the street and grab him. Two days ago, Saji had forcefully dragged him to Asiya's. Mehar hugged her son and made him sit on her lap. Already Saji had warned her: *Please do not cry. He does not like that.*

She kept asking him, 'How are you my dear? Are you eating properly? You have lost a lot of weight!' He said nothing. 'Why did you not come to see me dear – in a few days your holiday will be over and you will have to go away – you did not even come for one meal that your mother made?' Her eyes brimmed with tears but she took care not to cry so that she did not upset her children. Saji's warnings echoed in her mind: *It seems every time he comes here, there is crying. You and Nanni are always singing dirges.*

For some reason, Ashraf never looked at his mother's face directly. His head was bowed the whole time, his body covered in dust, his face visibly dirty. Even his clothes smelled of stale sweat. The previous night he had told Saji that he was going to visit their mother, and Saji had made sure that he took a bath in the morning.

'Hey, where did all this dirt come from?' Saji asked the question on Mehar's mind.

'I went cycling', he said this without lifting his head, his voice soft and sulky.

Saji sat in front of him staring intently into his face. She wondered what made him sit like that. Was it the fear that his father would scold him if he learnt of this visit to the mother? Was it the guilt of not having visited her all these days? Or was he simply angry with their mother? She could not find out so easily, but whatever his reasons, she felt pity towards her younger brother.

The fear that her son could be angry with her crushed Mehar. She felt even angrier with her own mother and with Hasan for bringing about such a situation where she had to be separated from her own children. But – without the words to articulate this anger towards anyone – she just kept sitting there.

'Please, please, eat at least two mouthfuls of food

and then you can go back to sitting.' Asiya's voice annoyed Mehar now. She didn't reply. She just sat there, totally pissed off that her mother had started her cringing manner of speech once more. Ashraf, who had been sitting quietly for ten minutes just grinding his teeth, made a clever use of this interlude to say, 'I'm going,' and ran outside before anyone could catch him. This made Mehar even more furious with her own mother. She had ruined the moment with this over-the-top display of sympathy.

An hour ago, Habibullah had called Asiya and said, 'Aunty, please keep your daughter with you. I'll be happy to be spared. Night and day, she was lamenting "My children, my children" as if mine was a home where death had taken place!'

He was calling after a month of Mehar's departure. He had not thought to call earlier because he was so upset that Mehar had left without even informing him. Neither Mehar or Asiya paid any heed to him. Even for this phone call, Asiya did not seem to be perturbed in the slightest. She just said, 'Okay, okay,' and then promptly hung up.

Nothing more could happen to Mehar, she thought. She had already faced the worst.

Mehar spent all her time until night fell staring into the distance. Ashraf did not even step in her direction.

She felt cheated. She understood that he had decided to use other roads to go where he wanted. She started weeping silently.

The school would be opening in a couple of days. She did not know when he would come again or when he might be on leave. She would have to wait until then. Saji was also leaving for her hostel.

CHAPTER 51

'I'm leaving, Kuppi,' Ashraf said with a big smile — showing off the gap where his front teeth had fallen out. Parveen hugged him close. She could make out that he was laughing only on the surface, and even his toothless smile could not hide the worry writ large on his face. For the last two days before she had left, Sajida had slept only on Parveen's lap.

Ashraf's body — held within her embrace — trembled like a twig. She did not have the heart to see him go. She patted him gently, 'Hey, why have you become like this? There is nothing in your body except bones. Do you even look like a boy of your age?'

He shrugged. He was enjoying the love he felt in his aunt's embrace.

'If you want to study nicely, you must eat properly when you are in the hostel. Read well and score good marks. Okay?'

She placed her hand on his head. 'Why hasn't your

hair been cut dear? Your scalp will sweat and you will catch a cold.' To this, he replied, 'This is the style, you don't know about it,' and he smiled.

'Get lost, crazy little boy! Not an ounce of flesh on your body and you are speaking of style.' Parveen gently rapped his head, poured him a glass of milk, and insisted that he drink it. Then she gave him a hundred-rupee note and asked him to keep it as pocket money.

'Did you visit Amma, little one? If you haven't, go tell her bye before you go. Isn't she the one who struggled hard to give birth to you?'

There was no response from him. 'I'm going to let you go only if you agree to this,' she said. Again, there was no response from him. She knew the extent to which Hasan had threatened Ashraf.

Once, she had asked her brother, *doesn't a child need a mother's love, why are you beating him this way!*

You shut your mouth and mind your business, and don't interfere with the disciplining of my children. Only if they are told that their mother has chosen the wrong path, will they grow up properly. What do women know? When a man does something, women must not interfere. You don't have to butt in here. Just go your way.'

She wondered why he always behaved so crudely. Whatever he talked about, he always finished with a final mention of Allah, Judgement Day or heaven and hell. Or it would be: *What do women know? Women should not interfere. Only men know.* She wished at some point he could realize how much hurt his behaviour was causing. And then she remembered that it was precisely this sort of behaviour that had caused her to live away from him, that had made Mehar leave him, and that had caused so much friction in his relationship with their mother.

Will women not have some wishes, beliefs, and thoughts of their own – or should their minds and hearts not exist at all? Why was he so stubborn in his thinking?

Everyone in the village prayed, everyone performed the Hajj. But it was only a few men of Hasan's age who were causing so much trouble to others, she thought to herself. As Ashraf left her with tears in his eyes, Parveen hoped and prayed he would grow up to be a better man than his father.

Sajida had started behaving like she was a young woman, no longer a girl. It was because she bore worries that far exceeded her level of maturity, Parveen thought. It was sad because the children were paying the price for their parents' and grandparents' mistakes.

Abida had been telling the others about the engagement of Mumtaj's daughter when Sajida was around. *They tied the sari to the girl and made her sit. She*

*was so so so tiny – there was nothing there – no hips, no fat
– why, she even lacked an ass. Her legs were just thin sticks.
And they covered her with so many jewels and wrapped her
in a silk sari – it was disgusting. And then we saw the husband. He is a real buffalo. So fat.*

*Mumtaj is tying a little baby calf to this stupid buffalo –
just because she is greedy for all the money.*

Saji had asked, 'Is it true that Mumtaj's daughter
Subi is going to be married? Really?' She couldn't
quite believe it was happening.

'I will study. Then I will take up a job. And on
top of that, under no circumstances will I get married,' she said. The severity in her words had shaken
Parveen.

—

Nowadays, it had become a habit for Parveen to
think about the BO whenever she felt depressed.
She laughed at the fact that just thinking of him was
enough to make her heart so light. Although the entire
situation appeared absurd, she wanted to believe in it.
The mind always waits to take interest in something

Nowadays, a man seemed to be necessary only to
fulfil the needs of the body. Although Parveen did
not need a man for anything more than that, her need
for physical love kept increasing. She felt the urge to

talk to him. But she did not have any reason to. For a second, she wondered if she should tell him about the wedding of Mumtaj's daughter. She really did not like the idea of the alliance. She somehow wanted to stop it, but her conscience did not allow her to act.

They had already fixed the date, they had printed the cards. It would be wrong to prevent it now. But, then again, they were performing a child marriage.

At the end of a long battle between rational thought and her feeling of guilt about betraying her own people, she called his number. Now she really had a reason to call him. The truth was that she did not want to let go of such an opportunity. She was aware of the complications at play here.

'Oh, there has been no sign of you,' his flirtatious tone made her heart race.

'How are you sir?' she asked.

'Why do you call me sir?' he protested. 'Just call me by my name,' he said, using the intimate singular.

'I missed you very much,' he said.

She was agitated – she did not know what to say. 'Oh,' she said. His speech made her blood flow faster. Then, with a great deal of effort, more intimately: 'How are you?'

'I'm good, thanks to your grace.' He sounded playful. A long dialogue appeared to unravel. Encouraged by the flirtatiousness of his tone, Parveen started to tell him. 'It's nothing. In my village, a marriage of a little girl is taking place. This Sunday. Please don't tell anyone that I told you, they will kill me,' and she immediately cut the conversation short, saying, 'I will talk to you later.'

Parveen was afraid she had done the wrong thing. She was confused and she blamed herself for acting in haste. Her throat was dry and her speech hoarse, so she tried to drink water to rectify this. She tried to cast the burden on God and to forget about all this. From Nanni's room, she heard a delicate cough and a long sigh. Then Nanni asked, to Parveen's utter shock, 'Who is the man you were talking to?'

CHAPTER 52

Amina Nanni felt perplexed as she paced up and down her own room. She walked in the direction of the bed and when she approached it, she stretched her hands out to ensure that she was near the bed. She sat down upon it, the soft mattress somehow comforting. She spread both her palms across the bed and smoothed the sheets like a little child. A dark room would certainly be filled with darkness. She grumbled to herself, 'What is the point of whether there's a light here or otherwise. I'm blind anyway.' She took her long hair and started to plait it. She recalled what Parveen used to say about her hair. *Allah, how much hair and look how black and shiny it is! Not even a single hair has turned grey, and look at me – I'm already balding and the few hairs on my head are going grey.*

'What is this old woman going to do with all this hair?' Nanni said aloud. She thought to herself: *could it really be true that none of the hairs on my head have turned grey. I am seventy years old — how is that even possible! Is Parveen making this up for the heck of it?* She did not know the answer to this.

She heard the sound of someone going past the street on a cycle. Her window was open so she also felt a surge of sweaty odour. It made her realize that her window had not been bolted shut. She tried to think of her life filled with sounds and smells. Right from when she could consciously remember she was navigating this world with her sense of sound. Her mother, her father, her relatives, the days of the week, the rain, rice boiling, the batter being ground on stone — she was aware of all this only through the sensory knowledge of sound and smell.

If she could smell meat either at home or on the streets, it was a Friday. It was the same if she could smell incense since the perfumed air of attar as the men walked past her house would indicate the jhuma prayers. She was able to discern the time just by following sounds. To this day, she had never asked anyone what the time was, nor what day of the week it was. Parveen often used to ask her how she sharpened her ears and her nose so well.

If she smelt parippu rasam, she would know that it was Thursday. Not only that, she could even comment, *the rasam is boiling but the tamarind has not yet been added.*

And then, she could greet people who came home just by listening to the manner of their walk. She could say, *come Nafeesa* based on her footsteps alone. She sighed. When she had come of age, she spent her days listening to songs on a transistor radio. For famous people like Shivaji and MGR, she had created her own mental imagery of what they might look like. By listening to the songs in which they appeared, she would curate their physical features. She had no clue how men looked – she only put together an idea based on hearing what others said. What was a moustache, a beard – until today she had imagined a man's body through her own interpretation – but because she had never known a man, she could not imagine him whole.

Flowers, leaves, vegetables, utensils, the stove, the grinder, the electric fan, the radio – she could comprehend these objects and their functions by touching them – but this was not possible with a man's body. As her mother said, at least she had an overactive imagination.

She had created for and by herself a notion of shapes and forms. Black, red, white, blue, yellow – she didn't know the colours. From listening to people around her she had gathered the knowledge that black

was ugly and white was beautiful. Fat was ugly, thin
was beautiful; short was ugly, tall was beautiful. Based
on the words that reached her ears, she created her
own imagery. These products of her imagination, she
designated as MGR, Shivaji and so on. She made use
of the longing in the voices of women who spoke of
how handsome MGR was, and used that to fashion
him.

Although these women – who were of a similar
age to her – were married and bore children, they too
had unfulfilled desires like her. For some reason, she
could not understand why this was the case. *I am not
married. But why are these women not happy? What's the
mystery behind all this? What man would even sniff a blind
woman even if she long hair and a pretty face?* It had been
a long, long time since she had forgotten the things
her mother used to lament. Even the wounds created
by these words had scarred over now, become numb.
But would the body and its needs follow in that direction – why did they not?

The sudden waft of flowers interfered with her
chain of thoughts – and she inhaled deeply. She felt
that the flower-seller Mumtaj was walking past her
house. She supposed that the flowers sold by Mumtaj
were in fact sweeter in their smell – all the same
regretted that she could not wear flowers now that

she was old.

When they were little girls, she and her elder sister Suleika used to love wearing jasmine. In a house without a father, when even getting a cup of gruel had been a struggle, where would her mother be able to afford buying flowers to pin daily onto the girls' hair? Yet still, every Friday, she would wash their hair and pin fragrant jasmine onto it. There would be many more flowers for Suleika, and very few for Amina because she couldn't see. One day, she had touched Suleika's head accidentally, and realized that she was wearing more flowers than her, and that her hair was in two plaits. This enraged her so greatly that she tore out the flowers from her own head, crying inconsolably. Suleika, who could not understand what was going on, ran to get their mother.

'Hey, why are you crying?' her mother screamed – but as soon as she saw the flowers torn and cast on the floor, she grasped what had happened without a word having been exchanged. How could a mother explain to her child her line of reasoning? *This is a blind girl,* she had thought, *it is enough to decorate her hair with a few flowers just for the sake of it – she is not going to look in the mirror and be able to see.* She had hesitated for a while and then said: 'Oh, it is nothing dear. Akka is elder to you and she is going to school. That's why I put more flowers in her hair. But you are only home my dear.' She pulled her to her lap and cuddled her. But unfortunately, this had made Amina cry even more. 'Why don't you send me to school too?' she wept. But her mother knew that it was impossible. She held her close for a long time. Her child could not see, she could not study at school, she could not see her reflection in the mirror and admire the flowers in her hair. How could her mother say all this?

She only knew the sun because she felt it. She could not know if the moon was out in the sky, if it was waxing or waning – though she would try to guess this based on what was being said at home. Her mother would speak of the birth of Venus, Suleika would say that the shining stars in the sky were sisters. And she would ask: *What does 'shining' mean? What do stars look like? What do the sun and the moon look like? Tell me.*

And Suleika would reply, *Shining means that it is bright, like a lamp. You know when a match is lit. That's how it is.* Amina wouldn't understand. The sun was a circle. The moon was a circle. But a star was different. That was when Suleika hastily realized that she could not explain what a star was like.

Circle – was that like a moringa drumstick, or like a brinjal? How did a matchstick shine? She would ask all these questions out of curiosity and ignorance, and her sister would struggle to answer. She would say things like, *Shining means shining*, or *circle means a circle*, or, *that's how it is!* – and she would rush into the street to play. She seemed to show a special enthusiasm for running away from her.

kuthadi kuthadi sainakka
kuninji kuthadi sainakka
kondaiyil thalampoo
minnuthadi dolaakku

Her voice would mingle with those of the children in the street. Amina would be left sitting on the threshold thinking up the answers to her own questions. She too wanted to run around and play like the others. But whenever she did go out to play, either someone would push her, or she would fall on a stone, and somehow she would come home with a broken toenail. It is said that an injury tends to occur in the same place – it seemed it was true. Now she had no nails on her big toes.

Her mother had made it clear to her. *You must not go out until your nails grow back. I'm already a widow – I cannot take care of your medical expenses on top of that.*

But she wanted to grasp how the sun looked. She wanted to know what happened to a match that was lit. She wanted to know what sight was. She had thought all this through for a long time but she had failed to come up with answers that satisfied her. She felt even worse when she thought that although Suleika had eyes that could see she could not even describe these things to her.

'Hold this in your hand,' she heard her mother's voice. She thrust a fruit into her small palm and Amina could tell by the smell that it was a guava. Her mother said, 'Hold it. This is how the sun and the moon are – round in shape.' She was trying to answer her daughter's long-standing question.

'Is this how it will be?' she asked with surprise and her mother hugged her. 'Yes dear. It's like this – huge and spherical. Though it will not fit into anyone's hands.' Now Amina also understood what a sphere was. She asked her mother, 'What is light and what is a star?' Her mother did not answer her and this confused her; she felt to herself that the light of a star must be a very, very complex concept.

One day, Suleika asked her mother, 'Wherever I go, the moon keeps following me – why does it do that?'

Her mother replied, 'Not just you, dear – the moon goes with anyone who is walking. That's because it's very large. That's why.'

That night, she thought for a long time about

all the things she missed because she could not see. When she was twelve years old, her mother had said to her, 'When you go to the toilet, if you wake up at night and your skirt is wet, and if it sticks to your thighs, come to me immediately.' She whispered this in her ears so that her sister would not hear. She told her this often, but before Amina could respond or ask her another question, her mother would move away. One day, when their mother was not around, she asked Suleika what it meant, what she kept telling her.

'What?' Suleika asked. Amina realized that her mother had not said anything similar to her elder sister. 'Okay, okay. Don't say anything to Amma. She will scold me for telling you.' Suleika could not make head or tail of it. She took Amina's hand in hers and said, 'Don't be afraid, I won't say anything.'

One morning, Amina was sitting in Chinna Pottu's verandah. Suleika had gone with the pot to fetch water. Amina would go to their neighbour's house without saying a word to their mother, feeling her way along the many walls. Chinna Pottu's house was the only house in the village that had a radio, and the radio would be playing very loud all day long because Chinna Pottu loved to listen to songs. She would go to the cinema every day to watch films. Her mother would say, 'Her husband lives abroad. She does not have any children. What else can she do?' But her voice would contain so much anger. Chinna Pottu would narrate the story of the film that she had watched that day. In this manner, she spread what she received.

Amina loved Chinna Pottu – she was not like her mother.

When the pleasant breeze caressed her body, reminding her of the time, Amina realized she was hungry. The street was filled with the noises of women and children. She realized that it was past the time for the azar prayers. She stood up and gripped the wall next to her. She knew even the exact steps to get back home – it was a path she had memorized.

'Hey dear, stop,' she heard the voice of Maimuna Akka. She touched her shoulder and said, 'Hey, you have come of age. Your skirt is red and drenched in blood.' And then she called, 'Amina's Amma – come here now – look at your daughter!' She heard the doors of her own house open and the footsteps of her mother walking towards her. She was standing there, confused, when she felt a resounding slap on her back.

'Idiot girl, you are sitting on the street and making it dirty – look all over your skirt, you are polluting everything. The whole street is gawking at you!' Her mother's voice betrayed her helplessness and tension. She grabbed Amina and dragged her home.

'Hey leave her, poor thing, she is but a small child,' saying so, Maimuna also came inside the house.

'Yes, you can say that. But I had already told this one. Don't go on the street, don't wear new clothes. Look, she is wearing the skirt and blouse that I had stitched for this Eid – and she's been sitting on the street – can I use this cloth again – shouldn't we throw away the clothes on which the first menstrual blood appears. I spent a total of thirty rupees on it.' Her mother went on screeching these unconnected exclamations as she dragged her towards the toilet behind the house.

Amina cried all day. She wanted to know the colour of the substance that was flowing out of her body and spreading onto her thighs. She knew that menses meant blood, and blood was red in colour – but she did not know what colour was – and that night she fell asleep thinking about this.

Now Amina was an old woman – and when she realized that she had not stepped out of her home onto the street since that day, she sighed with regret.

It was fine – the cultural conception was that a woman should not leave home until she got married – but what could she do? No one came forward to marry her. What could she do? She had to remain like a vegetable all her life – and that is how she had spent the last seventy years.

She had suffered so much to negotiate those days of her youth without being able to step into the world, without the touch of a man. To whom could she go now, and ask to find out what a man's body was like? Till today, it remained an open question. Today, Parveen's loneliness was not like the loneliness she had endured. There was the TV and the mobile phone. These could instigate her desires even more. It would become impossible for her to control herself or to always comply with the strict codes. Amina Nanni faced a dilemma as to whether she should ignore all this… or whether to confront Parveen about it.

She felt that she had to be supportive of Parveen beyond consideration of things like family honour and shame. It was an alacrity that went beyond all this which had made her granddaughter snap, after all.

CHAPTER 53

The village was in shock. Nobody understood what was going on. The police from the town, officials from the social welfare department and an advocate from the child welfare committee had all arrived and surrounded the home where the wedding of Mumtaj's daughter was to take place. The whole village had gathered to watch the argument between the officials on one side and the husband of Mumtaj and the jamaat chief Amjad on the other.

This is not fair, women said to themselves as they watched from the verandahs of their homes, secretly relishing the drama.

Amjad said, 'According to the Muslim law in our village we will marry our daughters at any age, at any time, as we please. The government does not have the right to interfere. Who are all of you to come here and explain the rules to us?'

He was fuming with rage, but constrained his

passion to show his authority in front of the community. In the middle of this tirade, he also went away
and made a phone call to a retired tahsildar whom he
knew personally.

The female officer was very harsh. It did not appear
as though she heard anything that anybody was saying. 'These are the collector's orders, that's why we are
here, the marriage must not take place, we will not let
it happen.' She spoke incessantly. Hanifa Hazrat was a
mute onlooker – he did not know what to do. From
inside the house, he could hear women crying. With
everything that was going on – the swaying plantain
trees, the aroma of biryani being prepared, the argu-
ments unfolding in front of his eyes – he felt dazed.
This was not good. He questioned himself: something like this had not taken place all these years, how
could it come to pass now?

As he combed his fingers through his beard, he listened carefully to what the lady advocate was saying.
She was quoting the name and sections of the law,
reeling out a list of the homes and villages where they
had stopped child marriages on the collector's orders.
She took out a folder with relevant newspaper clip-
pings, but seeing that Amjad was not paying any heed
to her, she closed it.

Hasan came now, shouting, 'Who has come here

to stop a wedding?' And Hanifa Hazrat thought to himself, *Ahaa, here he is. I was wondering why he hadn't come sooner...*

Amjad bhai's face shrunk. Hasan was always causing trouble, he thought. Asking for the balance sheet of the mosque's expenses, demanding that all financial transactions be written out on a blackboard visible to the public, and fighting every year that celebrating kandhuri was equivalent to assigning rivals to Allah. He could not stand the sight of this man, so he turned his face away. Nowadays, Hasan was not even praying in the mosque in their village – he would preach for hours, instead, about how the attitude of this moideen andavar mosque was against Islam. He himself would go to the tawheed jamaat mosque in the neighbouring village.

From his conversations so far, Amjad realized that nothing constructive was going to come of it. For half an hour, he had reasoned with these bureaucrats, but it did not yield any result. Worse, this was happening in the presence of the whole village – and now they would assume that he was incompetent. He was wondering how to avoid coming off as totally useless, but thankfully the arrival of Hasan made things more convenient for him. He told Mumtaj's husband Rasheed: 'Now I'm talking to them, let no one interfere without reason.' An implicit threat was contained in those words. Both Rasheed and the villagers knew exactly who he was referring to. Rasheed did not know what to do, he was perplexed and overwhelmed. 'Thalaiva, please don't abandon us,' he begged.

Hasan meanwhile was raging – he was shouting and picking fights with the officials like a boor. An officer said, 'There is no need to create a scene or to shout. If anyone interferes with our job, we will be forced to make arrests.'

Amjad thought over the situation. He himself was incapable of preventing the officials – this much was rather clear to him. He felt that instead of accepting this as his failure, he could spin the situation to make it appear that Hasan had made things infinitely worse, that he – Amjad – might even have been able to sort things out had he been left to his own devices. He felt a sense of relief that his personal honour might still remain intact by the end of all this.

But the fact that Amjad had stood apart gave Hasan even more impetus to behave brashly. He misread Amjad's intelligent manoeuvre as evidence of helplessness. By fighting with the officials, Hasan was intent on exhibiting his courage to the village in order to redeem the respect he had lost. This was his innocent calculation. The lawyer, in her striking looks – a single diamond nose stud, a high bun, and cotton sari – looked at his empty shouting with distaste.

The social welfare official used the maximum effect of his authority to address him: 'Mister, don't tell us what is said in your religion – you can go and say all that in court. None of you have the right to justify a child marriage. First, learn your rights.' His tone was powerful and indeed, it perturbed everyone, including Hasan.

But Hasan, in his foolishness, tried to hide his fear and raised his voice even higher: 'Don't bring your laws here, we have our own laws, don't forget that.'

The official seemed to have anticipated this move. He said, 'Mister, are you going to step aside, or should I press charges against you?' Clearly, he was ready to show that his team was prepared to act accordingly if necessary. This police official who was silent until this moment, went towards Hasan and calmly said, 'Sir, please don't create commotion here. Let us do our duty' – his face was peaceful but his voice was strict. He managed to convey to Hasan that he had to leave. Now Hasan did not know what to do. He understood that he had to admit his failure. He muted his voice and asked, deflated, 'Okay, so what do you want us to do now?'

Relieved, the official said, 'The girl's parents must give us a statement in writing that they are stopping the wedding – otherwise we will take the child into our custody and keep her in a social welfare home. We will have to file a case concerning the respective parents. Please decide as you wish.'

In tears, Rasheed wrote a letter saying that they would put a stop to the wedding.

But a couple of days later, the marriage was performed in secret in the middle of the night – without anyone's knowledge.

CHAPTER 54

A kind of gossip started to spread around the village. The idea was that it was Parveen who had informed the collector's office about the wedding! Parveen thought that this must be the handiwork of Nafeesa – but she felt courageous because the marriage had taken place anyway, and so she couldn't be blamed. The fear and the guilt that she felt previously was now gone.

She was able to work as usual. Although she did not leave home often, she made sure to visit Mehar and her mother. Mehar seemed to still be in a state of shock. The vacant expression in her eyes always upset Parveen – and she realized that Mehar only stayed alive because of Sajida's support.

The sound of Nanni crushing betel nuts disrupted her thoughts. *That woman has a rat's ears*, she thought. She had been surprised that within a second Amina had discovered that she was on the phone with

Moorthy. Whoever entered the house, she'd greet them just by the sound of their footsteps, whether it was Abida, or Rafeeqa, or Nafeesa. That's how sharp her ears were, Parveen thought to herself. Since the day Amina had questioned her, Parveen had stopped talking to the officer on the phone – now, she was in touch with him only through WhatsApp. She lived in a small house, and just from gauging the tone of her voice, Amina could identify who she was talking to. Parveen was afraid that she would say something to her mother, but nothing happened the way she had feared.

The sound of a knock on the door brought her to her senses – and she opened the window to see Hasan standing there. Because of the sudden nature of his visit, she grew afraid. In her mind, the idea had been ingrained that a visit from him was generally a bad portent.

She wore her headscarf and opened the door. He said his salaam, entered inside, greeted Nanni and sat down next to her. Parveen watched from near the door, her face brimming with disregard. What fresh hell would he bring now?

Like a ball that falls from an unexpected quarter, he asked, 'It seems you were the one who gave the tip-off about the marriage?'

She was absolutely distraught. Afraid of saying anything, she kept silent, frozen to the spot. 'I'm not talking based on guesswork like the rest of this damn village does. I got your phone bill from the office. It is an itemized bill. It is perfectly clear with whom you have talked.' Parveen felt that the stress on the word 'whom' was a giveaway. She hung her head in shame.

As far as Hasan was concerned, he was very satisfied that the standing of the jamaat's leader was finally reduced in the eyes of the village – Amjad was a good-for-nothing son of a cunt. Yet, he felt that the state should not intervene in Islamic law and codes. He did not budge from this perspective and he felt this was an uncompromising position to take.

Now, he was immensely pleased when there was no response from Parveen. He had come there only to announce that she was still under his supervision. Once that was done, he wanted to leave immediately. 'It would be good if you kept the honour, status and respect of our family in mind. It will be good if women remain women. Don't roam around in the name of a self-help group, or this and that – everyone in the village thinks badly of you.' He left after giving her this final piece of advice.

Parveen was equally shocked and irritated. It was humiliating that her brother was monitoring her by looking at her phone bill. It was good that Nanni had made that remark that day, she thought – it had made her act more carefully. Nanni who had heard everything Hasan said, gently spoke: 'He is doing too much! He is an idiot, monitoring who calls whom and when people go to the toilet.'

Parveen could understand that Nanni was trying to console her – but she was not in a position where she needed such consolation.

CHAPTER 55

Mehar was still lying in bed but her mother had decided to start the day by cursing Hasan and his second wife, as she had seen the two of them roaming somewhere in their car earlier that morning.

'How arrogant he must be to always drive through this very street – son of a cunt trying to make us jealous. Allah, please ask him – he has made my daughter sit at home, are You happy with the way he is enjoying himself in the meanwhile?' Mehar lay there, without being perturbed in the slightest. She thought coolly that it was because of Hasan and his second marriage that she faced all this destruction. Even when she had been married to Habi, she had dreamt of taking her children and living with him somewhere far away. Hasan had separated her from her children and ruined even that chance – and now he had managed to bring her back to this forsaken village. No one respected her here. She couldn't attend any celebrations in other people's homes because she felt too ashamed. All of this was a result of Hasan marrying again. And yet, he was able to roam around town with his new wife. He would not be made to feel shame simply because he was a man.

Her mother's anger had been ignited since the morning and it had taken the form of such harsh words.

The wife of Hanifa Hazrat stood by the window, listening to what was going on for a few good minutes, before she shouted across the verandah. 'Hey, why are you having a screaming fit? As if you have not done anything wrong – did your daughter actually need a second marriage? Will anyone now accept your scolding, will they take your side? Why are you storming like this? Just shut up.'

Just as her mother's crying and cursing came to a stop at that exact second, Mehar also understood that there was never a real end to any of it.

She wondered if there would ever be a peaceful solution to all this. If so, she could not figure it out. *At least I have an aim in my life. I wait for my children to come home and be with me. But does she have any solace whatsoever? She has assumed very clearly that her daughter's life does not have any meaning – so does she not realize my state of mind? Is the only life worth living a life with a*

man? Even I do not have any expectations about my life –
why does she punish herself thinking of all these things, she
thought.

Though Mehar tried her best to not cry now, the
tears of her mother tortured her – they were unbearable. She thought it an unsolvable problem and
wondered for how many more days, months and years
her mother was going to cry like this.

Sulaiamma said gently now, 'Leave it. What are
you going to do with all these tears – everything has
happened as per the will of God--only His plan will
come to pass. Do you think He is not aware that you
are crying and suffering?'

Asiyamma wiped her nose with the ends of her
sari and said, 'I have made puliyanam, please wait,'
going inside the kitchen.

'Yes, is the stomach going to know the state of
our mind?' said Sulaiamma. She peeked into Mehar's
room and shouted, 'Hey, get up and wash your face,
eat and come over to our house. If you remain in bed
like this, what else can your mother do but cry?'

But Mehar lay there, unperturbed.

CHAPTER 56

Parveen was very annoyed. It was humiliating to know that her calls were being monitored by her brother. She tried to rationalize his behaviour by reminding herself that it was natural for a brother to be concerned that his young and single sister should not be led astray. And yet, it felt utterly belittling. She felt sure in her knowledge that he was doing this because he suspected her of behaving immorally, seemingly because she kept going to the collector's office and to the banks. Then she wondered if her own behaviour would actually confirm his suspicions. And perhaps she was making a mistake? This thought, too, reared its head from time to time.

As far as he was concerned, women stepping out of the house was bad. He felt it was unsafe. So what was there to feel ashamed about, she thought. She also bought a separate prepaid SIM card, deciding not to share this number with anyone henceforth.

She felt relieved that Hasan could no longer monitor her – and proud of her independence from him. Why should he monitor her? Shouldn't she be the one deciding what she should or shouldn't do? How could someone else decide on her behalf? This feeling rooted deeply within her fierce heart. Even now, her conversations with the officer Moorthy continued under her new number. Because they both knew with absolute certainty that their relationship could never cross a certain limit, they both seemed happy to cherish what they shared. He taught her what it felt to be in love.

This was a feeling she had never experienced before, and she savoured the happiness that it brought her. But whenever she'd feel a guilty conscience, she'd suffer, too -- and for the next couple of days she would keep her thoughts contained. With the aid of the Quran and her prayers, she would try to chase away the shaitaan within. But in the next couple of days, her desires would reach an irrepressible point. The things for which she sought the forgiveness of the Lord just a few days ago would appear to her so guileless now.

The beauty and fragrance of love that was borne in her room, she always kept well-hidden from Nanni. But the spring in her step, the songs that she hummed to herself and the films she watched on television were enough for Nanni to sense what was going on. But Amina did not try either to monitor her grand-daughter or to control her. She seemed to enjoy it with a complicit silence. She knew that one could not always refuse the fruits of time and age. But Amina was keen that this should not go past a certain point.

CHAPTER 57

The pain in her legs was unbearable. She needed Hasan's help even to step down from the car. 'Be careful, watch out Amma,' he said. Her eyes welled with tears because he was talking to her again after nearly a year. She got down and slowly walked inside the house. He held her arm supportively and said, 'Take your medicines at the right time. We will have to go again next month.'

She sat down on the sofa and said nothing.

'Why can't you keep Parveen with you to help you?' he asked.

'But she must take care of Nanni,' she replied.

'You can bring Nanni here too,' he suggested.

'Oh no! Who can keep talking with her? She chatters constantly and I cannot keep up. Parveen doesn't engage with her nonsense, that's why they are able to carry on as they do,' she said.

He hesitated a little and then said, 'Do you want

me to bring Khadija here – she can help you around the house?'

'For what?' Subaida retorted with extreme anger. 'You do nothing of the sort. I will manage. The naseeb has been drawn on my forehead that even in my old age I should take care of your children!' Seeing his mother's face fill with rage and helplessness, Hasan quickly averted his gaze.

After a long silence, he decided to try and make a move.

On the way to the mosque, he saw Siddiq walking. He stopped his car and said, 'Why are you walking alone machchaan?'

'I'm on my way to pray, shall I join you?' he said, and opening the front door, sat in the front passenger's side. 'It's only on the next street, why do you drive to the mosque in your car,' asked Siddiq. 'If you walk there it will take care of your exercise as well.'

'I had to go into the town. It was getting late for prayers so I decided to rush back.' He passed across the main street to approach the mosque as a college bus went past.

'This bus takes the children of our village to college every day,' Siddiq observed. 'He starts at eight in the morning and comes back at five in the evening. Even girls who have come of age are going.' Then, in a conspiratorial tone, he added, 'Last week I heard something. You know the son of Dhandapani, even he takes this bus. And Khaja's daughter – the one who is still studying, I forget her name – it seems she is also going to the same college. Some seven, eight of our children are going in that bus and they saw that guy and this girl sitting next to each other on the same seat, laughing all the time it seems. What an age we live in!'

Siddiq's face had reddened, and it was evident that he was anticipating something untoward to come of all this. 'What will happen when we keep cotton and fire next to each other – anything might happen. These times are different. They look at the cinema and believe that it is real.' Hasan did not reply. He was thinking of his own daughter at college.

Not knowing the reason for his silence, Siddiq tried to change the subject. 'We must warn this jamaat of all this, and organize lectures for women every week. In the mosque we hear the preaching and the hadith but should it not also reach the ears of women and the children at home? They spend their time watching cinema, television, gossiping, creating tensions and on top of that, the biggest shaitaan is the phone.'

Hasan seconded his words wholeheartedly. He too was gripped by the same fear of modern, liberal culture. 'The jamaat leader isn't alright, machchaan,' he said. 'Does he even care about the village? He has that post for prestige reasons, that's all.'

They had reached the mosque, so they got out of the car and walked in silence.

Rashid and Razak were walking towards them, too. Hasan realized from their cold stares that they did not greatly appreciate that he had driven here in his car. As if they were challenging him, their stares said: *Are you feeling proud for having come here in a car?*

These days, he could identify some form of disrespect in the glances of several people. Even those who had once held him in high esteem and had feared him seemed to be talking to him only out of courtesy. Still. What could he do? Was it possible to go and ask people why they would not respect him? In his mind he thought they could all get lost, but in truth he found the situation unacceptable. He felt his blood pressure shoot up. All these people who would earlier offer their salaams – nowadays, they passed by as if they simply had not noticed him. It was an unbearable shame. He thought to himself, *Is it so wrong to marry a second time? I only did what was lawful and nothing that is impermissible. Did not the Holy Messenger do so, so what is their problem?*

Siddiq raised an eyebrow as if to ask why Rashid and Razak were giving such looks, to which Hasan gave a half-hearted reply: 'seems they are on their own path.' He moved towards the place where they could perform their ablutions.

He resolved that he would once again become respectable in the eyes of his community. He started washing himself with the water. It was cool to the touch. He came to this mosque only once in a while, and most people turned back to look at him. Most days, he would go the mosque of the tawheed jamaat in the next village.

Just as the azar prayers finished, he stood up and started to address everyone: 'Salaam alaykum. I want to remind everybody here of one thing. For some time now, women have not been receiving religious teachings at home. We are no longer living in the old times. Shaitaans like TV and mobile phone have entered our homes, and ibaddat has slipped away quietly through the back door. In most families, prayer has been reduced. If this jamaat can organize a bayaan once a week in a different home it would do much good. It would also be good if the women's madrassa were expanded. We should stop sending the girls to college, instead they should be sent to the madrassa and taught what is ilm. On TV, all they watch is the serials that keep running – so how can we teach girls what ilm is?'

Having said this with some anger in his voice, he sat down.

No one spoke. They gave each other blank stares. Amjad bhai sat with an irate look. He was wondering to himself: *What place is it of his that he's interfering with the administration of this mosque?*

He had the impression that the others were expecting him to reply. He could visibly see on their faces the eager anticipation of this leading to a fight, and their keenness to entertain themselves by witnessing an argument. A few looked at him with a pitying expression that said, *He has nothing better to do.*

Although Amjad bhai was grinding his teeth in anger, he swallowed his feelings and pretended to be calm. A few worshippers from the front row got up and started to make their way home – following them, the entire gathering dispersed, mumbling to one another as they headed home.

Hasan felt very disgraced. They should write a petition to the wakf board and remove Amjad from his post, he thought. He felt embittered. 'Look at the peaceful life this man leads, though he is a swindler who doesn't share details of the mosque's finances.' He walked towards his car.

'Let this village rot – why should I be the only one who cares?'

In three months' time, Sajida would finish her twelfth standard exams. She kept telling everyone that she wanted to become a doctor. He didn't outwardly approve of that, of course, women should not be so crass and ambitious – but he would be proud if his daughter was a doctor. She was also very good at her studies. Though this would mean that she would have to study along with men. He could not allow this. He was afraid that if she studied with men for five years, some sordid love story might develop.

He decided to enrol her in an Islamic college, he would let her get some degree and then marry her off to a pious young man. *I have to practice what I preach,* he thought. *I cannot tell the whole village how to behave and change my approach when it is my daughter.*

Khadija had also said, 'Your daughter is very arrogant. If she gets a big degree, she will never respect you.' He felt that this was true.

Look at the drama this uneducated Mehar bitch has caused. If she had been educated, could anything have contained her? Now, she has run away from the second husband as well – the stupid woman! He was furious! *And what about my own sister – she's not educated but she has got the guts to tip off the collector to try and stop a marriage. Things will be impossible if these women are not controlled.*

'Allah' he said, and sighed.

CHAPTER 58

Amina was applying oil to Parveen's hair, chiding as she expertly massaged her scalp.

'Do you ever take the time to take an oil bath, girl, all your beautiful long hair has gone!'

'Who cares that it is gone?' Parveen retorted.

Amina ran her fingers through Parveen's hair and remained silent. It appeared as if she understood the truth of her granddaughter's words. In her silence was a tacit acknowledgement, too, that this was a sad state of affairs. She kept working the oil through Parveen's hair.

Hasan had tried twice to find her a husband. Both men worked with him in the tablighi jamaat, and had even travelled with Hasan as part of their religious work. One was a widow with two children. A lot of people said he appeared rather Sufi with his long beard and all that – even though he was only from the next village – but Parveen had declined. 'I will not be someone's second wife and bring up their children.'

'But who will take you as his first wife?' her mother had asked her matter-of-factly.

As for the second candidate, he too was a widower. But because he did not have any children, Hasan felt that he was a serious prospect. When an opportunity arose, he said with a lot of pride, 'This groom is much more religious than me, he is even much more mindful of ibaddat.' Parveen decided then and there that she would not marry him. She understood with perfect clarity that this was just the sort of alliance that Hasan would bring along – and so she decided she would not get married again.

'She's so arrogant – how does she think she is going to lead her life alone?' Both Hasan and Subaida grew tired of arranging suitable prospects for her, blaming her for her stubborn pride. But because Hasan's ibaddat was impossible to bear, Parveen was now living here with Amina. She knew that if her husband behaved similarly, she would not be able to cope. She had witnessed first-hand what Mehar had to suffer. He was constantly chastising, constantly controlling. Parveen would not willingly choose that life for herself.

Nanni was also deeply absorbed in her own thoughts. She was upset that God had cursed Parveen with the same fate as her. Her anger towards Rahim's family grew like a flame. *They married this golden girl to an impotent man and reduced her life to nothing,* she thought. *Just as Subaida's life was ruined because of her marriage to Shahul, Allah has cast the same fate on her daughter as well.* In a hesitant tone of voice, she said, 'Can I ask you something, Parveen?' Parveen had been anticipating this for a long time. She had sensed the urgency with which the older woman's fingers worked her hair.

'Ask me, Nanni,' she replied.

She realized, from Nanni's still fingers that she must have been taken aback by her response. To make her comfortable, Parveen once again said, 'What is it – please ask?'

'Nothing... Will you tell me with whom you speak on the phone?'

Parveen felt as if Nanni's long words were crumbling and falling on top of her in pieces. She hung her head and remained silent. Nanni's small hands settled on her shoulders in a comfortable hug.

'Is he from the village, or from outside?'

This question was a bolt from the blue.

'Don't be afraid, I will not scold you. I will not betray you. Just out of curiosity. Even I was once your age, you know.' And as she said these words, tears fell from her eyes. Those tears were enough to leave Parveen feeling totally devastated.

Parveen shrunk with shame and sadness. Nanni tried to console her. 'Don't be afraid. It is enough to just talk on the phone. Just take care not to cross that limit dear. That's enough.' Her words were simultaneously a warning and consolation. Parveen saw her Nanni walk away, almost as if she was weightless.

She remained rooted to the spot for a long time thinking of the depth of Nanni's words – how she at once divulged her knowledge, her support and explained the limits of her permissiveness.

Parveen felt the long-carried burden of her fears melt away. When she realized she and Nanni were on the same wavelength, she was filled with a sense of liberation.

CHAPTER 59

For one whole week, Mehar had been suffering pain in the lower abdomen. Only yesterday, she had managed to see the doctor in town with her mother.

'There's an ulcer in her cervix. You put your daughter through so many abortions – now, look at what has happened.' The doctor was angry when she saw the scan and scolded Mehar and her mother.

Asiyamma asked with wide-eyed ignorance, 'How could it cause an ulcer now when the abortions took place four, five years ago?' The doctor was irritated by this suggestion. 'What do you know? You married her off when she was just a child and now you come and question me?' Asiya shut her mouth immediately.

'Okay, I will ask them to prepare the operation theatre. We can burn the cervix a little, otherwise she will get cancer.' She quickly instructed the nurse that they would be performing the cryosurgery promptly. Both mother and daughter exchanged nervous glances.

Seeing the fear writ large on their faces, the doctor said, 'It's nothing, it takes only five minutes, it's painless.' She did not let them spend another moment in deliberation, quickly moving on to the next patient. As Asiya and Mehar came out of the examination room, the fear of possible cervical cancer made them extremely worried, not to mention the medical bills and expenses this procedure would involve. The nurse was busy writing something down.

Asiya asked her softly, 'Ma, how much will this cost?'

The nurse was wearing a white sari and a white blouse. Her hair was tied up in a bun. She looked directly at Asiya when she spoke, 'It will be less than four thousand. You will be paying for medicines separately.'

Asiyamma had a little money with her. She had brought it along in the expectation that she could buy new clothes for both her grandchildren while she was in town.

'How much I suffer without a man – even you must be aware of it, Allah' she exhaled out loud, taking issue with the Lord publicly. Then she clutched her daughter's hand supportively, 'You please don't worry. They say that you can return home immediately.' She was trying to ease Mehar's fears. Mehar's face, already pale from anaemia, appeared even paler.

'No Amma, I'm afraid. We will come another day,' she pleaded. Asiya did not agree, the doctor's words were still ringing in her ears. 'No, no, let us do it now. It only takes two minutes it seems.' She tried to boost her daughter's morale, before quickly moving to the next counter to pay for the treatment.

After a giddiness that lasted half an hour, they returned home that same evening. There was no apparent reason for concern, and everything seemed to go well.

'There will be some minor spotting but it will go on its own,' the doctor had said. That night, Mehar felt an itchy sensation in the place where the doctor had given treatment. She grit her teeth and bore it. As time passed, the itching became more intense. She went to the bathroom and scratched herself. Blood ran. She kept scratching and scratching and the itch increased. The itch did not subside, and Mehar started crying in frustration. She grew worried and depressed that in exchange for the small problem of addressing her abdominal pain, she had returned home with a larger complication.

She got up from the toilet with some effort, found the copy of her prescription where she located the doctor's number and tried to call her. The first couple of times, the call kept connecting to an extension number and this made her cry even more. When she called again, finally, the doctor answered.

'What is the matter?' Her tone was harsh and it made Mehar even more anxious. 'Doctor, it is itching a lot, it is itching where I pass urine. I cannot bear it, it does not subside.' She started crying on the phone. From the other end of the line, the doctor said, 'That is how it is after a cryo. The itching will increase as the ulcer heals. If it is possible come here again.'

'No, I cannot go anywhere. It is horrible,' Mehar wept.

'You will find candida cream in the shops, try to get some and apply it. If the itching still continues, come over, and we can do the cryo again.' The doctor hung up.

'Fucking bitch!' Mehar shouted. She was angry. 'Here I'm suffering and she wants me to come again for the same treatment.' She doubled over and started to wail. She once again went to the toilet and started scratching. Her private parts were now swollen and red because she had scratched at them with her nails.

Her mother grew worried. 'Let us go there again to the same doctor,' she said.

Parveen purchased some candida cream from the

pharmacy. 'Apply this,' she said, 'let us see if your itching subsides.' She remembered that the tahsildar's daughter was a doctor. Although it was nine o'clock at night, Parveen called her in a panic because there was no other option. And besides, Parveen was respected among the officials and was seen as a favourite of the BO and the collector.

The tahsildar's daughter was the only female doctor nearby, and she worked in the Sivaganga Government Hospital. Parveen had heard that she returned to her village, a little distance away, every night.

The tahsildar confirmed that her daughter was home and asked the women to come right away, so Mehar and Parveen took a taxi, reaching there around 10pm. There was no sign of activity in the village at this late hour. The doctor smiled warmly upon seeing Parveen. 'Amma told me, come inside please,' she said. She was about thirty years old, and she had a beautiful, smiling face.

Mehar was suffering. It was miserable even to watch her sitting in the car in so much discomfort. The doctor read the reports and led Mehar to a small room.

Parveen had not brought Asiyamma along. She would have complained all the way during the car journey and made Mehar's condition even worse.

From the time she remembered, this was how Asiyamma had always been. She would shout, fight, curse. She would constantly be blaming or scolding someone – relatives, neighbours – she just had to find fault with someone or the other.

It was true indeed that her life had been full of hardships and sadness. But it was not as if the others in the village did not have any problems of their own. Still, Asiya always behaved as though she was the only one suffering, as though only she was wretched, abject. And the cause of her difficulties, according to her? Her godforsaken relatives and neighbours!

Once, when her pet goat died, she blamed a neighbour for casting an evil eye and caused a clamour on the streets. The entire community had called her a foul-mouthed woman. Parveen sighed. She looked around. The doctor's home was neat and beautifully furnished. Everything was in its proper place. *Look at our homes*, she thought. *No matter what, the educated people are different!*

Then she resolved that they must somehow make Sajida a doctor – just like the tahsildar's daughter. If Parveen and her sister-in-law and the girls they had grown up with had not got such an opportunity, at least Saji should. She sighed again, this time with disbelief.

She heard the door open. The doctor and Mehar emerged outside, one behind the other.

'The womb is indeed damaged – but the mistake was the cryo surgery, why did you go through with it? I cannot understand why they did it. Now the area is very ulcerated. On top of that, she has scratched with her nails and now it has gotten even worse. Even I don't know how she is coping with it.'

The doctor looked genuinely sad. 'I never recommend cryosurgery to anybody. It is horrible, these days they are using healthcare as a money-making racket.' Then she said, 'Please don't go to that doctor again. Add this tincture in hot water and wash your wounds, they will get better. More importantly, please keep your mind at ease.'

'I have the feeling something weighs heavily on her shoulders,' she said to Parveen.

Turning to Mehar she added, 'Don't be afraid, ma. It's nothing. Keep your mind at ease.' She patted her on the shoulders. Parveen felt that the doctor's name and nature went very well with each other. She had seen it on the board outside: Dr Shanti. 'Thank you so much, doctor,' she said and opened her purse to take out money.

'No, no, there is no need for all that. Have a good journey back. Mother has said a lot of good things about you.' Listening to her comforting words, both Mehar and Parveen felt lighter. Mehar's face, which had been full of fear earlier, appeared calmer now. Even at this moment, Parveen thought how, if she were here, Asiya would curse the other doctor the rest of the journey home – and it made her smile.

Parveen also felt that she had had a narrow escape with things – no one in the village knew for sure that it was she who had tipped off the officials. They could blame her indirectly, hypothetically, purely on the basis of their suspicions. But she felt happy and proud to be respected by the officials in the collector's office.

—

Early in the morning, Parveen was offering her prayers. The sun was still rising, but because she had gone to bed late last night, she could not wake up in time for fajr. Now, the fajr prayers had lapsed into the next prayers. She heard the bell ring, expecting it to be the milkman. She took the vessel and went to the door. It was Hasan, Parveen was surprised to see him so early in the morning. Perhaps their mother was unwell, she panicked – but if that was the matter, he would have called her. She was very confused. 'What's the matter, anna?' she said.

'Did you take that stupid bitch to the doctor last night?' he asked. His words burst violently like fire ants at night.

'Don't shout from outside, come in,' she said.

'For what? She insulted me – and Allah is punishing her for that. But look at you, you are on her side, roaming with her, like loose women. Be well.' He spoke angrily and left in a huff. She wondered how he must have learnt of the incident. The taxi driver must have ratted. *What a damned village,* she thought. She had told Ajeesh, the driver, not to say anything to anyone. 'That idiot has gone ahead and passed it on,' she grumbled to herself as she bolted the door.

The bitterness she felt towards her brother was unparalleled. He had married some other woman, brought her to the same village as his first wife, and justified it by saying it was allowed in Islam. And on the other hand, he had left his wife of many years and his children on the streets to fend for themselves, and today he was directing his anger towards them! What nerve he had! Well, his anger would not harm her.

She reminded herself of all the work she had to do today. After a long time, she wanted to call Moorthy again. She cherished him in her thoughts much more because last night's encounter with the tahsildar and her doctor-daughter had gone off so brilliantly. In part, this must be because Moorthy held her in high regard. She knew right away that she was treated in such a special manner, even by these relative strangers who were government officials, because they must have heard Moorthy sing her praises. It made her feel special to know that he was fond of her.

After Nanni had advised her, she believed that she had forgotten about him. But now the memories of him were multifold.

CHAPTER 60

Mehar felt healthy. All these days she had wanted to do nothing but cry, her pain had been so debilitating. Then the night after the cryosurgery, she had been in so much discomfort, she wanted to die. If Parveen had not taken her to the doctor, she thought she might have done something to herself. At that moment, she had not thought about her life or about her children – she had no memory of anything, could simply not conceive of anything beyond the pain.

Lying in bed, she scanned the calendar hanging on the wall. It was from Ratnam Stores. Because there had been an image of God on it, Saji had pasted white paper over it and on top of that, a photograph of herself and her younger brother. When she lay in bed, Mehar always looked at that photo. She was happy that the kids would finish their annual exams and be home in a week's time. This year, she had seen Ashraf a total of only five times. Whenever Saji came home during her holidays, she spent most of her time with her.

Once, during Ramzan, the children came to the village for four days. Hasan had forced Ashraf to also fast although that child was very frail. As a boy, he did not yet know how to take care of himself, nor when and what to eat, nor even the significance of fasting. When Saji tried to protest, Ashraf said that he could not object because his father would scold him otherwise.

Saji had said, 'He's not even eating enough at the break of the fast. I do not know why he is so afraid of his father.'

Mehar had replied, 'Your father had kept me in such terror as well – how will he spare his children?'

'Not possible with me. I'm not one to keep nodding my head to everything he says.' Hearing the resolve and confidence in Saji's tone, Mehar had been stumped.

This photo had been taken during that Ramzan. Ashraf had lost a lot of weight and had grown dark – his face appeared tired. The chudidhar that Saji was wearing was not beautiful at all. When Mehar asked Saji about it, she had explained: 'I had gone with Aththa but I did not understand which one to select. I picked this one out, but if you have been with me, it would have been better.' Her face had betrayed her helplessness and lack of experience – in so many ways, she was still a girl after all.

'What is Ramzan anyway? You are not with us, Aththa is elsewhere. It was just me and Ashraf with Nanni.' The happiness and excitement that must surround festivals for a child of that age had been totally missing from Saji's face. Mehar remembered how the neighbour's children were so thrilled that Ramzan, and all the while her own daughter was so sad.

When asked why she was not wearing a new sari, Mehar replied that she had not bought one. She was respecting the forty-day mourning period for a second time then, and had not wanted Saji to know about it. Habi had come back and obtained in writing her consent for a divorce. Now that, too, was settled. But this time, she was glad. She felt as if all the little devils that had followed her had finally left her to her peace. All the difficulties and humiliation that she had to endure in the name of marriage had been enough. She thought that Saji should not get married at all! In Ramzan, when she had decked Saji up in so much jewellery, Asiya saw had sighed. 'I took great care in picking out each piece of jewellery for my daughter's marriage,' she'd said. To be reminded of this at such a time irritated Mehar to no end.

Saji said, 'I am not going to get married. Please sell all this jewellery, I am going to study to be a doctor.' Her eyes had shone with eagerness, but Mehar could detect a hint of her worry that her father would not permit her to study.

'You read well my dear, I will give you all my jewellery, you need not get married at all,' Mehar's words rushed forth. Asiya scolded her, 'On an auspicious day, you are telling a child to not get married. Will any idiot do a thing like this?' she said. Mehar had mumbled to herself, 'So you still believe in marriage?'

Saji again said, 'That's not possible. I'm going to study and become a doctor.'

The thought that her children were coming back for the holidays made Mehar feel alive. The pain that she felt in various parts of her body betrayed the physical cost of what she had suffered all these days because there had not been sufficient blood circulation. Now, she was relieved that Sajida was not angry with her, but she still did not know how to handle Ashraf's taciturn moods. Hasan's constantly scolding had pushed him into some sort of confusion and anxiety. At whom could he get angry? Who was doing the right thing? These questions left him confused. This filled Mehar with dread and fear.

She understood that she would never again be able to live with her children; she would spend the rest of her days filled with longing. Nothing was in her hands anymore and it was clear that everything had gotten quite out of hand a while ago.

CHAPTER 61

The last exam for Saji was finally over. Her heart was filled with relief and silence. This was the most important exam of her life. The marks that she was going to score in this exam would decide if she was going to be a doctor or not.

When all the other children had gone home on their study leave in order to spend time with family, she had stayed behind in the hostel. Was it even possible to study when she got home? At her mother's house, she would only hear laments and wails. If she went to stay with her father instead, she would have to listen to his ceaseless advice and hear him curse her mother constantly. Who was bothered about her studies? They were all worried about their own problems.

These days, when Saji thought about her mother's decisions – including her decision to remarry – she found it surprising more than angering. Although it was true that to get married was idiotic, Saji wondered how her mother had such a capacity for resistance even though she lacked any education. She was even more in awe of Parveen. How could she summon the courage to tell Hasan that she did not want to marry again? His word was law in the household – and she knew for sure that to disobey him was indeed a very big thing.

She had rolled up her bed and had packed her bags. She was waiting for her father to come and pick her up. Most other students had bid her farewell, and hugged and left in tears after taking her address.

There was no one at the hostel whom she could consider a best friend. She had spent two years here without becoming specially attached to anyone. She knew that any sort of friendship would not bring her the consolation that she required.

The warden Laxmi used to often ask her, 'Why are you always alone my dear? You can go and play with the others, you can talk to them – why do you need so much silence at your age?'

Saji would only smile in response, almost as if to say, *What is the big deal in playing and laughing anyway?* The warden would look at her in sympathy, marvelling at how mature Saji was already at such a young age. Saji would pretend to be indifferent to such looks of pity.

If her father said he was going to turn up at three in the afternoon, he would turn up at six. That was how it always was. He completely lacked any sense of planning. It was now four o'clock. Saji was happy to be leaving behind the hostel's bad food, but she was caught up in the worry that for the next couple of months, she would be surrounded by a great deal of stress. If home was hell, where could she go?

She had to constantly be a witness to the complaints being raised by both sides. She was also not unaware of the problems that awaited her next May when she hoped to begin her further education. She sighed as she looked at the trees in the distance. In such a large school compound that stretched in all directions, there were only four trees. There were a lot of plants, but it would take years before they grew into trees. The oppressive heat that constantly surrounded the school and the hostel made her even more wistful. She longed to go home, lie in bed in her air-conditioned room and go straight to sleep.

What a life! She didn't like being here, and she didn't like going there.

Two suitcases filled with clothes, a bucket and a mug that she used for taking her bath – this was all the luggage she had. She decided she would throw away her uniform the minute she reached home. She simply hated that green and white combination. 'Which idiot selected this?' she rued. 'This ruins everything. All the other schools have uniforms in such smart colour combinations.' She made sure to look around now just so she could rule out the presence of the warden and her sympathetic eyes. She glanced at her watch – it was now five o'clock.

She had been waiting for two whole hours. At least if she loved the prospect of going home, the wait wouldn't appear so burdensome – but she felt simultaneously hateful and angry.

It had been almost a week since Ashraf finished school and went home, his body shrunken like that of a malnourished child. She thought of how many more years it would take for him to finish school.

When she thought of going back home, the only thing that filled her with happiness and made her look forward to it was being with him.

She had a pounding headache. This had become a common occurrence nowadays, possibly it was as a result of staying up most nights to study. She reminded herself to check with the doctor to see if she might need new glasses.

At some point, the sound of an approaching car snapped her back to reality. Because everyone else had left, the playground and the hostel were deserted. Her father got of the car, apologizing for his lateness. Sajida looked up at him. He was darker, he didn't seem to have the same face as before, now he appeared graceless.

She had planned to be angry with him for turning up so late, but she abandoned that idea. 'Please wait, let me put on the burqa and come back,' she said and walked towards her room.

'Aththa, we have to change my glasses. I'm getting headaches,' she said to him as soon as she got inside the car. Perhaps it would be possible to sort this out right at the beginning of the drive.

'Not today, another day,' he said, tired. He stopped at a Pazhamudhir Cholai on the way and bought for her a glass of her favourite orange juice. 'You have become very thin,' he said, 'You have been studying too much.'

'Yes, Aththa, only if I study very hard and get high marks can I join the medical college,' she said.

She waited to see how he would to respond.

'Only if you qualify on merit,' he said. 'You will score enough marks, no?'

'Pray for me,' she replied.

He took the glass from her hands. He purchased fruits from a vendor, a mix of oranges and apples, and placed one bag next to her in the back seat. 'Eat properly and improve your health,' he said. Then he placed the second bag of fruits on the passenger seat. One moment she had been melting from the love that he was showing her, and the next she was feeling depressed. The moment she realized those fruits were for his second wife, she hated him fiercely.

Did he have to do that in front of her? As if to remind her cruelly that there was another woman worthy of his love? She was angry with him but she did not say anything.

Not comprehending her state of mind, he asked, 'After getting into the car, did you say your prayers for the journey?'

'Yes,' she answered with absolute indifference.

For a while he was quiet, unable to work out the reason for the anger in his daughter's voice. Just to keep the conversation going, he said, 'Yesterday I sent your brother to the forty-day tablighi jamaat – if he stays in the village during the vacation he will just loaf about as he pleases. You know how he is.'

Sajida was shocked.

'My brother is not there, you have sent him away?' she asked in a rush of indignant words. 'Why did you send him away, when you knew that I was coming?'

He tried to ignore her rage and said carelessly:

'Why are you shouting? Don't you want him to prop-erly learn ibaddat?' He seemed annoyed.

'We are both studying in different corners, we meet each other only during the holidays, we look forward to spending time together, now you have ruined that by chasing him away. Now with whom will I spend my time?' She felt devastated and helpless as thick tears ran down her cheeks.

'Why? Did your mother brainwash you? Did she tell you that he should not be sent?' he shouted. 'You are saying it is wrong for him to learn ibaddat, and that it is enough if he just roams around. You are an educated girl! All this is indeed really doing you good, is it!'

As she opened her mouth to protest, he shouted at the top of his lungs, savouring this last cruel word: 'Just shut up, I know what is right and what is wrong for my children!'

After that exchange, there was no need to talk with him further. She was outraged that Ashraf – who did not get good food or care in the hostel – was now being dumped away for another forty days like an orphan. She pictured his earnest tears.

With her own tear-filled eyes and bitter heart, she thought now of her mother. She could easily figure out the sole motive behind Aththa's decision to send

Ashraf away: he had wanted to separate mother and son. She thought of the ways in which her mother and father were behaving in order to take revenge on each other.

When he had married again, her mother had prevented Saji from speaking with her father for six months. Even she was angry that her mother had done this. Sometimes, she had longed for her father, she wanted to speak with him, but she had remained silent out of fear of upsetting her mother.

After six months, her mother had said to her, of her own accord, *You can talk to your father if you wish.* Saji wondered what caused this sudden change of mood. *If even you won't talk to him, all his love will be reserved for his second wife, and he won't spend anything on you, he will squander it all on her. You can speak with him.*

And here, her father had transgressed from merely preventing his son from meeting his mother to sending him away. Saji felt that they were both being kicked around like unwanted toys.

By now, she had no interest whatsoever in going home. She closed her eyes, longing to go away somewhere far-off, a distant unseen place.

CHAPTER 62

Subaida did not know how to console Sajida who had come home in tears, refusing to eat, and now weeping miserably in her room. She herself sat in the living room, staring blankly at a shadow in the corner. The final call to prayers reverberated in a melancholy echo.

I prayed and prayed – but what has come of it? Subaida thought to herself. She was depressed. How much more sorrow was He willing to heap on her?

From the day of birth, all that had remained was sorrow. As far back as she could remember, not a single day has passed without prayers. There was not a good deed she hadn't done. And yet, God was making her family suffer so with his constant tests. *My husband was charitable, my son is the same. If anyone comes seeking help, isn't my son the first to help them out? And isn't my son the one who stands at the very forefront when they are building a mosque, a madrassa? And does Allah not have sympathy even towards him? He is only going on*

Your path, so why are You doing this to him? She openly chided Allah.

She realized that Sajida's sadness was legitimate. She had come back eager to see her little brother and now she felt cheated that he was not there. She, too, was angry at her son – why had he chased away that poor child for forty days – he was only small. Even in her old age, it seemed, she lacked peace! She had never expected that Parveen's life would be ruined in such a manner. And now, the manner in which her son's life had hit rock bottom made her feel as though she could never be able to come to the surface to escape all the sorrows that threatened to drown her.

She had tried various things to ameliorate her circumstances but they did not change at all. Knowing that she could not make Sajida eat or cajole her, she sent for Parveen. She was confident that once Parveen came, Saji would eat. She repeated 'Allahoo' as she walked towards the entrance of the home where she could do her ablutions. The pain in her knees was agonizing. Parveen had told her, 'Now that you are old, you must learn to live with the pain. Please don't take medicine as and when you please.'

Parveen, too, was disheartened. Making Sajida eat was no big deal but her heart couldn't bear the thought that Ashraf had been sent away. She knew that Saji would indeed find this unacceptable. If she, as the children's aunt, was feeling so sad and angry, she could not even comprehend how Saji and Mehar would feel about it.

Before going to the tablighi jamaat, he had been lying on her lap, crying, 'At least you tell Aththa, I do not want to go. I will see my sister when she comes. I will attend these classes for a week, but not forty days.' But Parveen had not been talking with Hasan since she had gone with Mehar to the doctor and he had come all the way to her doorstep to lecture her about it.

After Ashraf's lengthy pleading, she called Hasan on the phone. After exchanging greetings, he said abrasively, 'I'm about to pray, what is the matter?'

She said, 'No, it's just that I heard that you asked Ashraf to go to the tablighi jamaat. Let him go for one week only, forty days is a very long time. He is crying constantly. There is not a scrap of meat on his body. He cannot cope in this heat. At least if he stays with us during the vacation we can give him good food and improve his health.' She was genuinely concerned, but she was still aware that the response from her brother would be cruel and cause her pain.

His reply was immediate: 'I want to do something good for my child. I want my child to learn ibaddat.

That habit which does not change at five does not change at fifty-five. Your imaan is not strong today because your upbringing was not proper. Even today I pray to Allah for that, to strengthen your faith. You do not have to interfere with the upbringing of my child.'

After he hung up, Parveen was speechless. She hugged poor Ashraf. Ashraf wiped his nose with his sleeve and returned home.

Mehar called Parveen every day and wept inconsolably. Parveen had not a clue when Mehar would finally be able to stop crying, if that day would ever come. The stresses on her were unbearable and Parveen feared that something dreadful would happen to her.

Parveen knocked on Saji's door, peeping her head into her room. On hearing Parveen's lovely voice, Saji quickly clambered out of bed and held her tight. Both felt hopeful and comforted after that embrace. Subaida began her prayers relieved that her headache was subsiding. She felt as if a bird's nest had been taken apart. It appeared no one cared about another person anymore in this cruel day and age.

Tomorrow was a Friday. Even as she was in the middle of her prayers, she realized that she was supposed to go for the women's religious instruction at

Ayesha's home. She knew that Parveen would not come. If asked, she would say, 'I am happy with the hadith that I know. Please, you may go and learn some more.'

Subaida continued her prayer.

CHAPTER 63

Hanifa Hazrat had said that the classes for women would take place today at Ayesha's house, he had also announced this in the mosque at the end of the Friday prayers. Hasan considered this a personal victory.

For some reason, it was too hot to even contemplate the idea of sitting inside the shop. The heat arising from the bags of fertilizer and the chemical burn from the pesticide bags suffocated him. In the morning, Ashraf had talked to him on the phone. Someone had dialled the number for him, because he had been crying so hard. 'I will never roam anywhere. I will stay inside the house, please let me come back Aththa,' he had cried.

The jamaat leader also observed, 'He is not eating at all.' It had been fifteen days now, and even Hasan's pity was stirred. But considerations of sympathy would not help his son learn vital religious lessons. This was the age when children were corrupted, and all the evil shaitaans came together to spoil the mind. Only if Ashraf learnt about good and evil, heaven and hell, could he then stay on the right path. Pity would not help his child.

Saji was not talking to Hasan. She was still angry that her brother was not with her. She said that Ashraf was being sent to the jamaat only to separate him from his mother.

Even Hasan wondered if this was indeed true. Had he sent the child away for forty days merely to take revenge on Mehar? Otherwise, would he not have sent Ashraf for only a week or a fortnight as everyone else in the village did? He had overlooked his own happiness of being with both his children, of Saji's happiness of being with her brother – and it had to be acknowledged that his hatred and anger towards Mehar had driven him to take this decision.

He silently looked out onto the street, he looked left then right. No matter how vindictive he felt, he also wondered why all of this happened, why he had to undergo so much sorrow. 'There is not a day when I don't pray, there is nothing I do which veers from His path. Why does He heap so much sorrow only on my family?' And then, he consoled himself by saying, 'Allah indeed does test the devout in this world.'

He was testing his faith, Hasan thought – whether

it was strong enough. After all, the imaan that he had, not even a speck of it existed among the women in the family. All that went wrong was a direct consequence of this, and he had no doubts about it. After all, his mother was seeking all kinds of quacks to remove black magic, and it was Mehar who had boldly given him notice of divorce. The reason for all of that had happened was because they did not accept everything as Allah's naseeb, the will of God.

He was firm in his belief that Allah was just.

Again, the memories of his daughter came to him. He reminded himself of how much she loved him. Her address, her affection – he missed the intimate manner in which her words to him signified a mixture of entitlement and love. It had been a long time since he had heard the warmth in her voice. Now, she called him on the phone as if it was a chore. He knew for certain that she did indeed love him, but he was also sure that this love had changed irrevocably somehow, the old love was no longer there.

He reminded himself of how happy he had been that his eldest was a girl. If the same child was sad and angry at him, he knew that he was entirely to blame. For some reason, this thought pierced his heart and there were tears in his eyes. He was eager for a future where his daughter would be less upset with him.

How to win her back? He thought about the fact that she wanted to study and become a doctor. No one in the village had done such a thing.

If she was to pursue medical studies, she would be studying alongside men. Would that be acceptable? Obviously, it wouldn't be practical. He had to enrol her in some Muslim college, or madrassa – and then arrange her marriage.

Again, he thought girls must not be given too much space to stray, it was dangerous.

CHAPTER 64

Mehar's health had deteriorated significantly. She had lost her mental balance for a while, since around the time Ashraf had left to join the jamaat. Often, she would lament to herself or shout at the wall. It was Sajida who stayed by her side and gave her strength. 'Where is our younger brother going to go? I will look after the matter. You don't weep and worry so much.' She had not anticipated the extent to which this would affect her mother's health. Nothing could console Mehar, and she firmly seemed to believe that her son hated her. When he came back she wanted to prove to him that she still cared for him, that she would spend the rest of her life repenting for her mistakes, that she would never again abandon her children. Saji planned to bring him over and also to release him from the grip and fear of their father's tyranny.

Over time, the anger she felt towards her father solidified into bitter hatred. Every time her mother wept, she felt herself harden even more.

Sajida had been anxious since the morning about her results. She knew she would pass the exam – getting a pass was not so difficult. But it was important to be on the merit list. The fear that it might not happen had caused her great fear and anxiety over the last two, three days. This morning, she had woken up, finished her fajr prayers and was now waiting for the result.

Her hostel-mate Geeta checked the results online and called her: Saji had scored 1,000 marks.

When she realized that she did not get the high marks she had expected, she immediately gave up her dream of studying to become a doctor. She knew that there was no one to pay donations to medical colleges and secure a seat for her. If she did not have family problems and if she had taken her papers without being consumed by stress, she would certainly have scored higher marks. She might even have got a seat under the state quota. Now everything had come to nothing.

The warden and the class teacher used to say, *You read so well, we are sure you will get a seat on merit*. What did they know of all she was going through?

Saji tried hard not to cry, but she could not bear the feeling of loss. Without her mother's knowledge, she wept and wept at her grandmother Subaida's place.

—

Later, when she went to get the transfer certificate, she remembered what her father had said. 'It is okay, you can join some college for a degree, don't be very upset.' Her class teacher had said the same. But Saji felt that it would have been better if she had failed. She knew secretly that her father was in a delirious state of happiness.

The teacher had been telling him, 'Brilliant student. We thought she would qualify on merit. I just cannot fathom... They used to say that from time to time, she would be sitting depressed in her room in the hostel, that's why she has not scored so highly...' As the teacher kept talking Hasan's face was devoid of any emotion. She had assumed that he would express some kind of regret, but Saji could see the expression on her face darken as she realized that talking to this man was pointless. Saji was embarrassed.

When they got back into his car, Saji sat there silently. Although her classmates Viji and Sandra had obtained less marks than her, they already had medical college seats in Karaikal and Pondicherry because their parents had paid huge donation fees.

Unable to bear her disappointment, she rushed to

the terrace of the building and cried her eyes out. Her heart refused to be consoled. Now, it would be her father who would decide which college she would attend, and what subject she would study. Under no circumstances would he pay heed to what Saji thought about the matter.

Parveen Kuppi said, 'I spoke to the tahsildar's daughter, she says that Karaikal is not so expensive. She also says one can complete studies from China or the Philippines – and that a lot of children in the neighbourhood are going. But your father must allow you first, what to do?'

'Think of something and apply for it, the dates might have already passed. Do you want to do engineering or something else?'

Saji told her that she was not interested in engineering. Both of them knew perfectly well that Hasan would want to send her away to a madrassa. They sat with their heads in their hands. Without a thought, as she twirled her dupatta around a finger, Saji said, 'I will study zoology if I can get an admission.'

'Okay,' Parveen's face brightened. 'Tell this to your father, get an application form and then proceed with things. He does not like anyone else interfering,' she suggested.

Saji was not afraid to tell Aththaa what she wanted

– but she was concerned about how to make someone like him, who had no idea of what higher education entailed, understand what she wanted. Filled with apprehension, she picked up the phone. 'Aththa, I want to study zoology. It is only being offered in two colleges, please will you get me enrolled?' she said. He really did not know anything about higher education beyond the terms 'doctor', 'engineer', and 'BA'.

'Okay, okay,' he said, 'I will make enquiries. We can get the forms.'

Sajida did not know how to proceed beyond this, so she remained silent and hoped for the best. It was difficult to be at home during these two months of leave. She was bored. And she worried about her future, panicking over the possibility that she might not be sent for further studies at all.

Parveen kept asking her what her father had said, seemingly even more disappointed with the news than Saji herself. 'On seeing the tahsildar's daughter, I so wanted to make you a doctor' – she said this at least four or five times a day, with a mournful sigh. What was the point of such lament?

Sajida's classmate Shivani, who could not afford to study to become a doctor either, had joined a bio-technology course in Coimbatore. Saji felt perhaps it would be good if she, too, joined a similar course. She thought of each and everything to the point where it would confuse her even further. This made her immensely tired.

—

Finally, Ashraf had come home. After offering the morning fajr prayers at the mosque, he entered the verandah, hugging Saji close when he saw that she had been waiting keenly for his return. Subaida, too, embraced him and kissed him on the forehead. He had become thinner and even darker still. The shadow of a thin moustache-like line had appeared under his nose, and his voice, too, was transformed.

Subaida was listening disinterestedly to the siblings' conversation about their respective results. 'You don't worry that you are not going to become a doctor. Join some other nice course,' Ashraf said, trying to give Saji some consolation. When she did not reply, he grew sad. He did not know what to do, so he sat looking at her worried face. Finally, he said, 'Okay, put on your burqa. I will take a shower. Let us go and see Amma.' He knew what he had to do to alleviate his sister's misery.

When they got to Amma's, the two children sat side by side next to their mother on the sofa. Mehar stroked their limbs lovingly. Parveen and Asiya were sitting at the threshold of the house. Ashraf's sunken, thin face was a pathetic sight to behold: he had passed the annual exam, and in a week's time, he would have to go back to the hostel. Saji sat with a heart full of disappointment. Asiya looked at her daughter and her granddaughter. She turned towards Parveen and said, 'Why should the girl study? We can get her married in two years' time. We need to make her healthy, look at her now. She has no chest, no hips, no breasts. What is a girl going to do with all that education anyway?'

Although Saji wanted to retort angrily, she was too weary to pick a fight. Parveen exploded: 'You idiot woman. Only because your daughter is not educated is she confined to a corner here, and I'm alone and sitting at home. Your time has long gone. But Saji's life awaits her. Please keep quiet when it comes to our girls' future.'

Saji was pleased. While she and Parveen Kuppi were dealing with the question of whether or not she would be allowed to go to college, here Asiyamma was adding another dimension to the problem.

Ashraf was lying with his head on his mother's lap, listening in silence to the women talk.

Saji was very happy to see her mother enjoying the presence of her son. Indeed, she was so immersed in her own bliss that she did not say a word. She realized the reason for Ashraf's ease was that he had gone for forty days without his father's hateful preaching filling his ears. Saji was relieved that at least one worry was out of the way. Yet, anxiety about what awaited her filled her with dread.

'I do not know what Aththa is thinking,' she told Parveen. The admissions period for college will be soon over. The seats must have all been allocated by now, and still I have not applied to any college. Whenever I ask Aththa, he just says, "Don't worry, you can definitely join, I'm in touch with the right people…"'

Parveen asked, 'But what has he decided now? Do you want me to make some enquiries for a college seat? If the dates go by, then you will only be staying home like the rest of us…' Parveen's voice betrayed her angst. She did not want Saji to be denied the opportunity to pursue further education.

'I don't know, Kuppi, I don't know what he is thinking. What can I do?' In her face which must have been filled with childish helplessness, Parveen could only see responsibility and worry that far exceeded Saji's age.

'Yasmin's daughter Ashika has joined BA – every day the bus comes to our village. Seems she will go and come back.'

Parveen immediately responded, 'No, no, that is no good. If you travel 120km every day, your body will be very, very tired. You won't be able to study properly.' Even Parveen knew that seven girls from this village were enrolled in college. They went in the same bus and came back every afternoon.

The other day, Yasmin and Nafeesa had been talking about this. Yasmin had said, 'I enrolled my daughter in college so that she could learn to speak four words of English. Tomorrow, if she gives birth, it will be easier for her to teach her child. Even if she gets married to a Dubai-based or Kuwaiti husband, it is a matter of pride if she can speak a few words of English.'

'Yes, yes, are we going to send our daughters to work? If they learn English they can teach their children and help them with their studies. We do not even know the ABC. When we go to the bank and see the others converse in English, I want to pull my tongue out and die. Shame!' Nafeesa laughed. Parveen had felt the same. She used to feel very disturbed about her ignorance – but what could she study at this point? Once when Moorthy was talking to her on the phone, he had talked in English on another line to the collector, and she had heard the conversation for a little while and yearned to be able to do the same.

Sitting there now, under a deluge of conflicting emotions, Parveen said, 'You don't worry. I will also talk to the tahsildar madam.' She started to make her way home, and seeing Ashraf resting at Mehar's lap was overcome with contentment. Happily, she donned her burqa.

CHAPTER 65

Hasan was unable to take any decisions, he simply could not understand what he had to do. Seven, eight girls from the village were going in the college bus every day, and he wanted to send Saji along. Saji did not agree. 'I cannot travel back and forth daily,' she said. Moreover, she insisted that she would only read zoology, whatever this was.

A Muslim women's college had been set up in town recently. Hasan had heard that the college combined both conventional studies and religious education. Hanifa Hazrat suggested he enrol her there – she could study and, at the same time, her religious education would qualify her for the title of alima.

Saji's response was clear: 'I wanted to learn to be a doctor, that did not happen. Let me enrol into a biotech or zoology course. Those are my interests. I'm not interested in studying just for the pretence of studying. I need to find a job afterwards.'

Hasan was enraged by this. Both the courses that she had specified were available only in co-educational institutions where she would have to study with boys. That was not something he could bring himself to permit. Given these modern times, what could he do if she fell in love, or some such calamity happened? On top of all this, what could be done if the boys got to look at his daughter. He mulled over all this and decided that if she was going to study it would have to be in an Islamic college with a madrassa, or she would have to stay at home.

He could not come to terms with the idea that a woman could go to work. If Parveen and Mehar, who were both uneducated, could behave so arrogantly and ruin the family's reputation – what would become of this girl once she acquired an education. He was pissed off.

He thought to himself, *Sajida has become too haughty – if I had sent her to a madrassa instead of putting her in school she would not behave so wilfully, she would have been obedient and pliant.* He decided against consulting with her. *If I take the right decision now and put her in an Islamic college, things will be just fine.*

He was satisfied with this decision. He called up Hanifa Hazrat who knew the principal of the Islamic college very well. It had already been two weeks since

the course had started but he felt sure that this recom-
mendation would ease the admissions process.

CHAPTER 66

Saji was not feeling very well at all. She was depressed that her dream of becoming a doctor had come to nothing. She had worked so hard, she had scored good marks, but it was still not good enough – and she was enraged at her father. She loathed him.

She shivered as she recollected the difficulties she had to undergo just to be enrolled for an ordinary degree in this college.

'Why does a girl need an education? If you have to study the course you want to study, you will be learning alongside boys. So you need not study any shit. Let her just go to college, the one I recommend – let her get a degree, and then let her be married and be done with it.' Her father's cruel shouting had made Saji's nerves shatter.

Subaida, who was chopping the vegetables, had said: 'What are girls going to do by getting educated? If she falls in love with some boy and runs away, what can we do? We would die of shame. And what could we do if she loved a kafir?!'

Hasan's face was red with anger. His words made Saji feel humiliated and disgraced, and she knew her Nanni was only saying exactly what her son wanted to hear.

No Aththa. I will not do any wrong, I just want to learn, she had sat at his feet and wept and wept. He did not appear to take her opinion into account. He took her transfer certificate and locked it up in the bureau. 'Don't be arrogant like your mother. Join a good college and you can qualify as an alima.' After he left, Saji had cried for a long time. Without her grandmother's knowledge she used her phone to dial Parveen Kuppi's number and asked her to come home.

Parveen came – fought vociferously with her mother, took the certificate out of the bureau, took Saji, and started home. Subaida started to wail loudly – she did not want Saji to study further and she was petrified that Hasan would come and argue further with his sister. But Sajida knew exactly who would stand up for her and help her realize her deepest dream.

Because the tahsildar madam had been kept in the loop, Saji was able to join the zoology course. Parveen brought Mehar and Saji to the college. They had decided to take this step because they were unsure if Parveen was legally entitled to sign Saji's admission papers. They thought it would be better if her mother was there as a parental representative. The three of them purchased all hostel essentials from a nearby shop, and Saji stayed in the hostel that very night. Everything appeared like a dream. Saji was very relieved that she was finally joining a course of her own choice. Mehar returned home, crying.

After her admission, all of Hasan's anger had now turned towards Parveen. He had stopped talking to Saji these last two months. Now, even during the holidays, she did not leave the hostel to go home. She had stopped talking to her father entirely. She could not understand what was so wrong about wanting to pursue an education. She was baffled by all his reasons and explanations about what was proper and improper.

Twice, Parveen came and took her to the village for the weekend. But knowing that Saji was back at her grandmother's place, her father did not come there. Subaida said, 'Why dear, your father put you through twelve years of school. You can study as he wishes you to. Don't you know how sad he feels that you do not respect him?' She was weeping.

'Even now, if you apologize and tell him, he will

get you admitted in the college that he has chosen. You are a darling, why don't you tell him so dear?' She sat at Saji's feet and begged her, but Saji did not know how to answer her, how to explain. She grew annoyed and decided it was best not to come here again.

'Because of you,' Subaida continued, 'your father was in a temper with Parveen and he shouted at her. She will not come here now.' Saji heard a dog barking in the distance. She sat there without reaction, as if she was numb. No tears could shake her now.

Parveen said on the phone, 'If your father does not talk to me, does it prevent the rice from boiling in my home? Leave it. It is nothing new.' She added, 'Your job is not to worry about all of this. It is just to study.'

After that Saji stopped going to her village. Some weekends, Parveen and Mehar would visit her instead. Although her strained relationship with her father was difficult to bear, Sajida tried her best to ignore it.

CHAPTER 67

Hasan was like a man possessed. He was not prepared even to believe that his daughter had disrespected his wishes. How was that possible? How could such an occasion take place? He could not accept it at all.

Hanifa Hazrat scolded him to the point where he finally came to acknowledge how Sajida had been allowed to behave so wilfully. 'What is this? A disobedient child. How can a girl child have so much arrogance? All this started because of your behaviour, who asked you to marry for the second time. Did Allah ask you to do that?' Embittered, Hasan had gone to Parveen's house, shouted at her vociferously, and then returned to his own gloomy thoughts.

I am a man who preaches to the entire village, and now my daughter studies in a college where boys also study, how they will mock me. Anger and shame tore him apart. He wanted immediately to put an end to her studies. Like a heavy smoke, this desire to prevent her studies filled up every aspect of him.

He could not see a way forward. Did she consider her studies more important than her own father? Did she not worry that he was no longer talking to her because her behaviour disgusted him so? All these thoughts ran through his head.

He was the man of the house, but the women had disrespected him and done as they pleased. They had utterly humiliated and belittled him.

The fact that his daughter, too, had slipped away from his grip was a reality that he just could not bear. *What wrong have I done to any of them. I treated her like my own life. Is there anything she has asked for that I have not bought for her. Haven't I done everything that a father ought to do? How could she forget it all?*

Yesterday, Siddiq asked him to his face. 'What machchaan. Your girl, I heard she went and joined college as she wished, it is difficult if she has to be in the same class as boys, ask her to be careful. You preach and counsel the whole village, but our own kids are not listening to our teachings.' Although he had said this casually in passing, these were words that Hasan simply could not bear to hear. He thought that God had now pushed him into a position where anyone in the village could ridicule him.

Sajida was not even coming home – she was happy

to stay in the hostel, even during the holidays. And all the while his heart was filled with fear and sadness. The fear that she would fall in love with some miscreant boy now transformed itself into a great sorrow. He felt tortured by the fact that his daughter was out of his control and by the fear that something untoward might happen.

Parveen was not bothered by Hasan's concerns. She thought that he was torturing himself and torturing others because of his own foolishness. If there were a thousand students in a college, were they all going to fall in love and run away? What idiocy. 'Let this whole village go to ruin!' she would say.

Why did he have such a blind superstitious belief? Had anyone else in the village tortured themselves or their family over such a matter? she wondered. Who did not pray, who did not follow ibaddat – there was always some gap between word and deed. How to understand this man, how to rectify him? She could not understand.

Parveen knew what pain it would cause him to not be speaking with his daughter. But who could solve that problem? Their mother was heartbroken because she could not bear the difficulties Hasan was going through. Parveen had stopped visiting when she started blaming her. *What do you think a girl is going to achieve by getting educated? Why did you have to do such harm to your brother? Obstinate girl!*

Meanwhile, Mehar spent her days eagerly waiting for the vacation that followed the quarterly examinations.

After a long time, because it was Bakrid, Saji was heading home. Parveen had come to accompany her on the bus journey home. The heat was stifling – slowly, Parveen started to talk.

'How are your studies? Is it difficult at college?'

'No way. It is very easy. I was a science student at school, so I find all this pretty easy.' Her face was somewhat darker. She smiled, but there was none of the happiness and prettiness that should accompany her age – how could there be? Every day she was filled with the sadness that her brother had been isolated from everyone who loved him. Parveen thought of how her brother had separated himself from the children, distanced himself from her. *How is he going to live, for what is he going to live, for whom is he going to live?*

Sorrow choked Parveen. Saji pretended not to notice and averted her eyes by looking at the road instead. The bus had not yet left. Because it was almost empty, the driver was waiting for some more seats to be filled up. Two white people took pictures of the bus stand and the shops and the people going by. Then they took several more of a turban-clad man drinking at the tea shop. They must have felt that the turban on his head was special. The man in the turban was proud and posed for them happily. He was at least fifty years of age. He knew he was not going to be able to see the pictures they were taking, still, he posed for the camera gladly.

Parveen remembered her childhood years. When she was about eight years old, she accompanied her mother to a wedding in Sivaganga. In the middle of their journey, they got down from the bus and waited for another. Her hair was in two plaits and she had flowers pinned into it, she wore a purple skirt and blouse. At that time, two white people got out of a car and started taking photos of the bus stand and the thatched roofs of the shops and the tea being poured in the tea shop. When they started taking her picture, she started striking poses for the camera. She put her hand on her hips, she put a finger on her cheeks – and they too had kept smiling and clicking.

She had been so, so happy that day. She had been pleased to think that they were taking her picture because she was beautiful. For some reason, she remembered this now.

'Hello Amma, you are here?' a voice pulled her into the present, and she noticed that Rasheed from their village was on this same bus. Because she was wearing her burqa in a manner in which her face was visible, he could recognize her – and he started talking amiably. Saji was wearing her burqa so her face could not be seen. Parveen said, 'I'm taking my brother's daughter back home. It's her holiday.'

'Oh, okay, okay,' he said and took a seat across from them. 'The heat is killing,' he grumbled to himself, fanning his kurta. 'Hasan has a car, doesn't he – then why are you suffering like this by travelling in the bus?' he said. The entire village knew that Hasan was not talking to his daughter or sister – so this impertinent question annoyed Parveen to no end. 'Just like that,' she said and brought the conversation to an end.

It was true, she thought. Why did Hasan punish his own daughter so. What was this fool living for?

The heat in the bus now slunk into her heart. When it finally set off, she tried to shut her eyes and sleep. Saji had taken Parveen's hand in hers.

When they entered Subaida's home, they were greeted by the voice of the wife of Hanifa Hazrat. Parveen said in a clipped tone, 'You stay, I will come later.' Saji understood that Parveen did not want to talk to Sulaiamma.

'Okay,' she said.

'Come here dear,' Subaida Nanni called her and

hugged her. 'Sit down,' she said. Saji removed her burqa, put it on the back of a chair and sat on the sofa. The house felt like someone else's. She knew that her father would not be visiting these days while she was here. Parveen had told her that Ashraf would be returning home that night.

'How are your studies going?' Sulaiamma asked.

'Good,' said Saji abruptly. Her face revealed that she was knew what was coming next.

'Your father does not like it, then why are you causing trouble? He is willing to enrol you in another college, please agree to it. He came and pleaded with me to intercede,' she said. Saji understood that Sulaiamma was here as a messenger. She worked out that this must be her father's doing or Subaida's. She just sat there like a statue, not replying.

'It's your fate, his fate. As Allah wills,' she sighed and got up to leave.

Saji understood that he was not going to talk to her. Overcome with sadness and anger, she quickly got up and went into her room, slamming the door behind her. All her suppressed anger was let out in that single door slam.

Saji stayed in her room, crying long into the afternoon until Ashraf came knocking. She dried her eyes, opened the door and hugged her little brother.

'When did you come? You have become very thin!' he said.

'No da, only you have grown thin,' she replied.

'What about you! You've grown thin like a mongoose. Look at yourself in the mirror,' he said.

'The food in the hostel is horrible. It is possibly better to even fast. At least we will be rewarded for it,' she said, tongue-in-cheek.

'Okay, let us eat. Nanni is calling us, and father has got me new clothes, come and see,' he said and pulled her hand to lead the way. 'After we eat, we can go to see Amma. We can even sleep there tonight,' he said. She didn't reply, she simply followed her brother.

Subaida Nanni had laid out the food on the table. She had made the chicken which Saji loved. Brother and sister sat side by side and started eating.

As she pulled on her veil, said bismillah and took her first bite, tears fell from her eyes onto her plate. She wiped them away and forced herself to eat. Her eyes fell on the sofa opposite the table. There was a violet-coloured chudidhar there that she knew for certain was not bought by her father because he knew she hated this colour. She understood that Subaida Nanni must have bought it.

She ate in silence.

That night her mother was applying henna on her

hands. Seeing the sorrow on her daughter's face, she gently said, 'You can talk to your father dear, I know that you cannot remain without speaking to him.' She said this in the softest manner possible. She knew that these days anything could make her daughter erupt at any minute.

'No, it is not necessary. I won't talk to him.'

Saji burst into tears. She shook violently as she sobbed and sobbed. Ashraf was shocked to see her cry so forcefully, his little heart could not imagine what pained his sister so.

Mehar did not know what to do. She simply embraced her daughter.

Hasan's disapproval was inflicting a deep wound into her child's heart. This much, Mehar understood. But she could not see how she could rectify the situation, and still pursue her purest dreams. She knew her daughter, too, was troubled by the question of whether this was a permanent state of affairs – or whether something would give.

CHAPTER 68

Sajida was travelling to her college, accompanied by her mother, Mehar. She was at the halfway point in her three-year course. She wished time would fly faster.

At the college gates, she was shaken by her mother's disappearing form. Slowly, she made her way towards the hostel. She decided that henceforth this college compound would be her only existence. She also swore to herself not to give up on her dreams for the sake of anyone else's wishes. The early morning sun rays tickled her eyes.

Last year at Ramzan, she had met her mother and father separately. This Bakrid, her father hadn't come to meet her at all. Ashraf said that he had not come despite Subaida Nanni's protestations. 'Leave it di, we will look after that, you study well,' her younger brother consoled her as if he was much older and wiser. The anger of her father was still something that she could not fathom.

Only confusion remained with Saji, because she was in a position where she did not know what great offence she had committed. She was worn down when she thought of other students who did not have such concerns, who could concentrate in peace – but she had to deal with so much tension and stress. If any male classmates came towards her, just to talk, she pulled her burqa closer over herself and walked away – not out of fear, but because she did not want to give any basis to the fears and obsessions of her father. All the same, she was determined not to give up her dreams at any cost – no matter what happened, no matter who feared what, or who decided what. She made her way to her hostel room with confidence and renewed vigour. She had a spring in her step, and as she walked on the floor that reflected the soft light of the morning, she felt that she was leaving firm footprints behind.

Two-and-a-half years divided her reality from her dream. She was aware of the time and of the path she had to take. Sulaiamma reported what Hazrat Hanifa had told her father: 'My granddaughters are studying in Saudi Arabia. Did Allah say that you should not study? Why are you so adamant, then?'

She knew that her father's entire objective was

to keep his daughter under his control. She clearly understood that to achieve his ends he would do anything and that he was waiting for the first instance at which she would do something wrong. Right now, all that he needed was just one mistake, one slip-up. That was enough, that would allow him to stop her studies and bring her home, under his control. *I said so already that this would happen. Now you see, it has happened. Just as I said.* Something had to happen so that he could later claim that he had predicted it all along.

What foolishness! What stubbornness! He wanted it to happen so badly, for his one fear to come true, to come to pass. In order to not let it happen, for his grand wish to go unfulfilled, she did not talk to her classmates. There were many days when she avoided going out with any of her female friends – and it was a source of enormous depression and bitterness. Last week, there was a college trip to Munnar. And then again, the chance to participate in the college day functions. Although she felt eager and excited, she refused to participate in both. Like a hermit, she watched her friends buy new clothes and pack their bags. She bottled up her feelings until the college bus drove away, then let loose all her pent-up desires, shutting the door and sobbing wildly.

Unlike them she did not have all these modern

clothes. Neither did she possess their happiness.
Or the family, and the love and support that they
all seemed to have. The feeling that she had been
ostracized made her sink deeper into sorrow and inferiority. When she started crying explosively, she had
the relief of emptying out all of the pain and bitterness within her. Whenever she met anybody, it had
become normal for her to compare herself to them
and to fret about it. When she saw her roommates,
when she saw their parents arriving together to meet
them, she felt absolutely crushed.

Whenever her mother turned up to visit her, the
others would ask: *Why does your father never visit you?*
Unable to answer their questions, she'd be filled with
shame. It did not matter how well she tried to hide
it. They must have surmised by now that her parents were not together. It was mortifying. They never
asked her anything directly; and yet, from the way
they looked at her, and the way they treated her, she
felt an undercurrent of sympathy and it took a great
deal of effort on her part to simultaneously tolerate it
and ignore it.

You must not tell lies, for Allah will beat you. This was
a lesson that she had learnt from her father as a little
girl. Now, she had to lie to her friends every day – and
she had to remember each of her lies so that there was

no scope for discrepancy. Time had trained her in this art, but she felt extremely uncomfortable about it.

When her roommates went away, she would wear their jeans and their sleeveless t-shirts and kurtas and look at herself in the mirror. In those moments, she thought of the photo album of her mother and friends. Even if they were old photos, it was always amusing to look through them. She had first dis-covered it while looking for something else in her mother's cupboard. Her mother at fifteen. Striking in bell-bottoms and a very loose full-sleeved shirt. Her eyes covered with sunglasses that hid half her face. Photos with their hands on their hips, in an effort to pose stylishly. Blurred photos. Darkened photos. Photographs with their heads cropped off. Looking at them made Saji laugh.

'Amma, what's this one, you are looking like a scarecrow here? And here, are you trying to look like a blind person?' When she asked these questions, her mother looked at her with a little shyness and then said, 'This was taken in those days when I had come of age and was still at home. When we saw actresses in the movies wearing different types of clothes, we too wanted to dress up. But where could we go for the clothes? Jessi's mother would bring the sunglasses, the shirt and trousers that belonged to her college-going brother, and a Nikon or some other camera, I forget its name. She was our next-door neighbour, you know. On those days, when Nanni wasn't there, the two of us took turns wearing the clothes and taking pictures.' Mehar sighed. In the end, she did not even get the chance to wear beautiful saris.

It was true. For as long as Saji could remember, she had always seen her mother in saris that were heavy and shapeless as blankets. With a black burqa. Everywhere she went that's what she wore.

Talking of those pictures, Mehar would say, 'Oh, the trouble it took for us to get this film roll developed! No one should come to know of it. Especially, it must never fall into the hands of men, it would be a matter of disgrace. At that time, an Anglo-Indian girl would come every day to teach English to Yasmin Kuppi at her home, and she was entrusted with the task of taking it to town and having it washed. We felt that the whole experience was an adventure.'

Today, trying on her friend's clothes, Saji felt the same sense of shame and adventure. She removed the jeans and t-shirt of Viji that she was wearing presently and put on her own chudidhar and a very baggy top.

Being alone in a room without anyone else to distract her made her despondent, and she dwelled on the past. She was haunted by her mother's anaemic face, by her brother's skin-and-bones frame. She wondered if the darkness she felt was like the darkness that lay lonely and scattered across the long corridor. The stillness of the trees outside her window, and the thick shadows disturbed her. She tried to think of a time when she travelled in a car with her father, mother and younger brother. That day had ended like a dream. Although that happiness had dissipated into nothingness like smoke, she had not learnt to control her dreams. She knew that it would take time to rein them in. It was only in her dreams that she could ever again travel with both her parents in the same car. So she would think of those long-dead times and make herself happy. This was how she brushed aside her disappointments.

Asiya Nanni would say, without ever growing tired of using the same metaphor: 'like a sparrow's nest was plucked apart.' It was true though. She had lived with her mother, father and brother as if inside a little sparrow's nest. Who had destroyed it? That Khadija bitch. Anger raced through her. She was outraged that a woman who had once nothing to call her own, and was standing around in street corners, had now reduced her mother, her brother and herself to dire straits. She felt bad that she used the same words as Nanni. She hated herself for being so full of hate and bitterness and rage. How many dreams had come to an end? Her dream to become a doctor has come to a stop. She felt a sadness almost impossible to bear.

At the end of her school year, when her father had come to visit her in his car, he had said, 'Khadija has said that you should not be allowed to become a doctor. Your daughter does not have enough restraint, she will spoil your name.' The words were like a slap in the face. No matter how much she tried to bury this deep, to swallow it and forget it, her anger and sadness refused to abate. She felt crushed, she wanted to weep. How much she had cried and cried. And yet, her anger remained irrepressible, it refused to be contained.

'Hey, your phone has been ringing for a long time, have you gone deaf?' Viji's voice brought her out of her reverie. Mumbling something that came to her at that moment, Saji stood up and reached for her phone on the windowsill.

It was her mother. She was frightened. What could it be about? Her delay in answering the phone must already have sent her mother into a panic attack. 'What happened? Why didn't you pick up the phone for such a long time? I was scared.' To soothe her mother, Saji went straight to the point. 'Why are you so agitated. Tell me.' Her mother's behaviour was not out of the ordinary, nor was it something that she had to feel concerned about. So, she just waited for her mother to tell her why she had called.

'Jessi. It seems she was talking to a man last night. The whole village is now in a state of high tension.' Her mother's voice was a whisper, and this pushed Saji into unbearable shock. 'Really Amma, what are you saying?', she asked, shaken.

'Yes, it is true. They beat up that boy and then dragged her home. Instead of coming home from the madrassa, that bitch went straight to meet him. My first thoughts came to you my dear. You don't have to study. Come back. I will not let you study any more. I'm so frightened for you.'

Her mother's voice contained an inconsolable anxiety and panic. Saji could feel, for the first time, that someone else's actions could perhaps bring her own education to a sudden halt. She felt as if her insides were on fire, and equally, as if she was floating apart from her own body.

Dulled, dissociated, instead of responding to her mother, she simply switched off her phone.

First published by Kalachuvadu Publications as மனாமியங்கள் (*Manaamiyangal*) in 2016.

Translation copyright © Meena Kandasamy 2020

This edition published in the United Kingdom by Tilted Axis Press in 2020. This translation was funded by Arts Council England.

This book has been selected to receive financial assistance from English PEN's "PEN Translates" programme, supported by Arts Council England. English PEN exists to promote literature and our understanding of it, to uphold writers' freedoms around the world, to campaign against the persecution and imprisonment of writers for stating their views, and to promote the friendly co-operation of writers and the free exchange of ideas. www.englishpen.org

tiltedaxispress.com

ISBN (paperback)   9781911284468
ISBN (ebook)   9781911284451

A catalogue record for this book is available from the British Library.

Edited by Saba Ahmed
Cover design by Soraya Gilanni Viljoen
Typesetting and ebook production by Simon Collinson
Printed and bound by Clays Ltd, Elcograf S.p.A.

Supported using public funding by
ARTS COUNCIL ENGLAND

ENGLISH PEN

ABOUT TILTED AXIS PRESS

Tilted Axis is a non-profit press publishing mainly work by Asian writers, translated into a variety of Englishes. This is an artistic project, for the benefit of readers who would not otherwise have access to the work – including ourselves. We publish what we find personally compelling.

Founded in 2015, we are based in the UK, a state whose former and current imperialism severely impacts writers in the majority world. This position, and those of our individual members, informs our practice, which is also an ongoing exploration into alternatives – to the hierarchisation of certain languages and forms, including forms of translation; to the monoculture of globalisation; to cultural, narrative, and visual stereotypes; to the commercialisation and celebrification of literature and literary translation.

We value the work of translation and translators through fair, transparent pay, public acknowledgement, and respectful communication. We are dedicated to improving access to the industry, through translator mentorships, paid publishing internships, open calls and guest curation.

Our publishing is a work in progress – we are always open to feedback, including constructive criticism, and suggestions for collaborations. We are particularly keen to connect with Black and indigenous translators of Asian languages.

tiltedaxispress.com

@TiltedAxisPress